BOBBY BRIGHT'S CHRISTMAS HEROICS

BY
John R. Brooks

ILLUSTRATIONS BY
Dan Daly and Troy Gustafson

Tate Publishing & Enterprises

Published by Tate Publishing & Enterprises, LLC
127 E. Trade Center Terrace | Mustang, Oklahoma 73064 USA
1.888.361.9473 | www.tatepublishing.com

Tate Publishing is committed to excellence in the publishing industry. The company reflects the philosophy established by the founders, based on Psalm 68:11,
"The Lord gave the word and great was the company of those who published it."

Book design copyright © 2008 by Tate Publishing, LLC. All rights reserved.
Interior design by Lindsay B. Behrens
Illustration by Dan Daly and Troy Gustafson

Published in the United States of America

ISBN: 978-1-61663-725-5
1. Children: General   2. Juvenile Fiction: Holidays & Festivals: Christmas
10.03.12

Special Thanks To

My wife, Lisa, and 11-year old son, Remington, who have continued to be my sounding board, not only in the first book of the series, *Bobby Bright's Greatest Christmas Ever,* but in *"Heroics".* I can only hope and pray they will continue to assist me in the next three exciting books in the Bobby Bright series.

Dan Daly and Troy Gustafson, outstanding animated artists, who left the movie industry to teach their remarkable skills and trade to college students on both our east and west coasts. Just some of their amazing Hollywood credits are listed below.

Dan Daly——————-The Lion King, Mulan, Lilo & Stitch, Brother Bear, Pocahontas, John Henry.

Troy Gustafson——Mulan, John Henry, Lilo & Stitch, Brother Bear, The Hunchback of Notre Dame

Tate Publishing, whose genuine interest in me, from the outset of our relationship, was extremely meaningful, along with the fact they loved my good buddy, Bobby Bright.

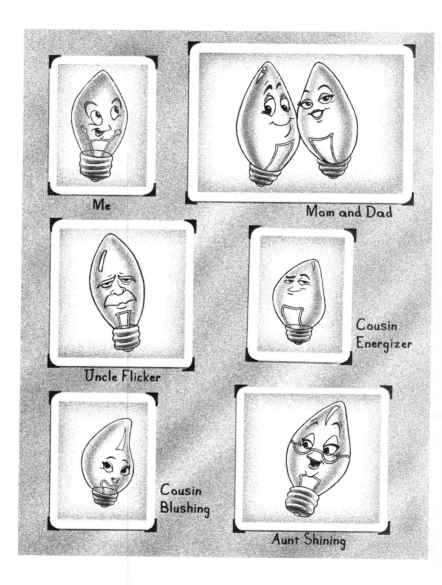

Contents

Our Family Picture

<u>Prologue</u>

Three Days after last Christmas

It was quiet downstairs. The clock in the foyer had just struck 12 noon.

The McGillicuddys had broken all tradition. They always took the Christmas tree down December 26th. But this year had been different, because Remington and his parents had extended their annual Christmas visit for two extra days. That meant both Christmas trees had remained up so the McGillicuddy's grandson could enjoy them.

Bobby Bright could hear the McGillicuddys talking in the far distance. He knew they had been taking down ornaments and strands of lights off of the big tree downstairs since around nine o'clock when Remington and his parents had driven out of the driveway to head back to their home many miles away.

Soon Bobby and his family would join all the other strands of lights that were on the big tree, and all of them would be placed in a storage box downstairs. Then it would be another 11 months in the closet, except for a couple of days when the box would be removed for Mrs. McGillicuddy's annual spring-cleaning.

It was a sad time, but nothing like each of the previous years when Bobby and his family had spent the entire Christmas season stuck on the back of the McGillicuddy's big tree, shining into a bare wall and seen by no one. This year, though, had truly been a miracle, and Bobby knew his magical powers had made it possible.

After all, shining brightly and making people happy was the job of a Christmas tree light bulb, and even more so if you were very special bulbs. There was no doubt Bobby and his family were important because Bobby Bright was the world's only talking bulb who could understand human language, and the other bulbs in his family were the only bulbs in the world who could actually speak among themselves in their very special language, Bulbese.

The bulbs visited about the good times and some of the funny things that had happened and were enjoying a good laugh when they heard Mr. McGillicuddy clomp, clomp, clomp up the stairs.

He quickly unplugged the strand from the wall socket and pulled it through the branches, before wadding the cord into a big ball.

After taking the tiny tree outside to the trashcan, Mr. McGillicuddy returned upstairs and scooped up the lights, and immediately clomped back down the stairs.

In the foyer, sat the storage box the McGillicuddy's used for their Christmas tree lights and a few select ornaments. Mr. McGillicuddy dropped the strand of lights on top of the box and walked away.

"What's happening, Bobby?" The questions came from everywhere.

"I can see inside the box, Bobby." It was his Uncle Flicker.

"What do you see?" Bobby shouted.

"All the other bulbs are in the box."

Bobby could see Uncle Flicker at the very end of the twisted cord, nearly hanging inside a hole that was formed by the four top sections of the box.

"Is every strand inside the box, Uncle Flicker?"

"Yes, it looks like it. But there may not be much room for us. As far as I can tell, they are all there, but it's difficult to be sure because there is a large white towel covering part of them."

It took three or four seconds, but suddenly it all made sense to Bobby, and he let out a loud, *"Yahoo! Good news, everybody. We are on top and separated from the other nine strands underneath. That means we are being saved to go on Remington's tree again next year."*

The bulbs started to cheer, but Bobby quieted them. *"Here he comes!"*

And then, what seconds earlier had been good news, turned bad. Bobby would have all winter, spring, summer, and fall to remember what happened.

Mr. McGillicuddy reached down, picked up the huge box, took three steps forward, balanced on one foot, pulled the door back with his other leg, then suddenly tripped, and fell forward. The box flew out of his hands spilling strands of bulbs across the floor.

Mrs. McGillicuddy was in the hallway and heard the noise. She raced into the foyer and yelled, "Look what you have done! Oh, John, you are the biggest klutz ever."

Mr. McGillicuddy did not move.

"Get up," she demanded.

He lay covered with lights, and stretched across the smashed box. Strands were wrapped around his head and arms.

Had it not been such a mess, it would have been downright funny. But for Bobby Bright, buried in a tangle of bulbs and staring at his family intertwined with other strands, it was anything but funny.

If they had been left at the top of the box, Bobby was certain they would have returned upstairs again next Christmas. But now, with lights scattered across the floor, the McGillicuddys would never recognize which strand had been on Remington's tree.

This had been "Bobby Bright's Greatest Christmas Ever," but would there ever be another?

PART ONE

1

Spring-cleaning at the McGillicuddy's

Jane McGillicuddy had never missed spring-cleaning during the many years she and John McGillicuddy had been married.

That was the reason Bobby knew the time was approaching, because, as he did each year, he had been counting the days until spring-cleaning as he lay in the middle of the big storage box in the closet.

For the first nine years of Bobby's life, it had always been difficult, because only the smallest flicker of light could penetrate past the other strands of bulbs and down to where he and his family lay, separated from the floor by only the cardboard bottom of the box.

If it was a dark, dismal, winter day outside, then there was no light; however, the majority of the days still produced enough sunlight that somehow the brightness would find its way through the McGillicuddy's dining room window, around the corner of the room into the foyer, under the bottom of the door, and, finally, into the closet.

It was there, Bobby Bright, the world's only Christmas tree light bulb who could understand human language, stayed with the other twenty-four bulbs on the Bright family strand.

In order to keep track of the days as they slowly passed by, Bobby had to be aware of that little ray of light. Whenever it disappeared, Bobby knew it was nighttime.

He could then go to sleep, but he also knew he had to make sure he was awake the next day, so he could see the miniscule glow again and keep track of the days as they slowly crept by through the rest of winter and the early days of spring.

Since Bobby was the smartest bulb, he was in charge of keeping track of time.

It was Mr. McGillicuddy's accident last December, just three days after Christmas, which had changed everything.

In a hurry to keep from being scolded anymore by his very angry wife, Mr. McGillicuddy had shoved the lights inside the closet. He put some in the box, but left at least half of the ten strands twisted and scattered across the floor, looking like they would never be untangled again.

Bobby had actually ended up more than halfway down in the box. Three strands lay beneath him. There were also some bulbs on top of him.

Some of the Bright family bulbs hung over the side of the box and spilled onto the floor. In other words, it was a total mess.

But even so, it was still easier for Bobby to keep track of time than it had been in previous years. He could see the small rays of light more clearly.

Counting days was very important. It helped getting through the long wait. And it was worth it, because as each day passed, it meant they were closer to a brief vacation from the closet, which they often called the "dungeon."

The vacation normally happened the first week of April. Since Bobby knew there were 96 days from the day after Christmas until April first, he always calculated that somewhere around 100 days Mrs. McGillicuddy would shout to Mr. McGillicuddy that it was time for spring-cleaning to start.

When that happened, the box, along with other items in the closet, would be pulled into the foyer where it would sit for two days while the McGillicuddys went about the chore of cleaning the house. It was a special time for the bulbs. They enjoyed the warm light shining into the box and their brief escape from the dark closet.

This year, though, had been different, since the McGillicuddys had broken their long tradition last December and waited three extra days before storing the lights for another year.

Now, if Bobby had counted correctly, today was the 99th day since the bulbs had entered the closet.

However, nothing had happened, and as the last dim ray of sunshine that had squeezed into the closet disappeared, Bobby said to his mom and dad, *"I guess it's time to get some sleep."*

But less than a minute later, he heard a sound that made him realize he had miscalculated.

It was Mrs. McGillicuddy's voice. "John, it's time to get the Christmas box out of the closet. I'm coming that way with the vacuum cleaner."

At that instant, Bobby realized this was the day he and the other bulbs always waited for. He had thought it was evening, but he had been mistaken. It was actually very early in the morning and the time of day when Mrs. McGillicuddy always started her spring-cleaning.

2

Out Comes the Box

"**G**et ready, everybody," Bobby shouted, "Spring-cleaning time is here!"

Cheers rang out from the Bright family lying twisted among the other strands.

In the distance, Bobby heard Mrs. McGillicuddy's voice. "John, where are you?"

"I'm on the way. Give me time."

"Time I don't have today. You know how I am. We need to get this house in order," Mrs. McGillicuddy said, as she marched into the foyer.

"Yes, dear, I know. We always have to be up by 6 o'clock so we can make sure all the dirt we're getting rid of doesn't get any sleep either."

"Oh, I feel so sorry for you, John," Mrs. McGillicuddy laughed and continued, "You have it so bad. Next thing you know you will actually have to start cooking your own breakfast and getting out of bed before 10 a.m."

Bobby heard the handle turn and saw Mr. McGillicuddy fling open the door and flip on the switch.

The moment the light came on, Mr. McGillicuddy saw the horrible sight and immediately remembered last December when he had clumsily fallen to the floor and bulbs had flown everywhere. He remembered his wife running into the room and finding him stretched out across the floor and covered with the twisted strands. And, yes, Mr. McGillicuddy remembered her exact words and her definite instructions, too: "You are such a klutz, John. You put everything neatly into that box before you put it in the closet."

"Oh, no!" he gulped. "What a mess! What was I thinking when I left the closet like this?"

"Did you say something?" Mrs. McGillicuddy called from the bedroom hall.

But before he could say anything, she turned on the vacuum cleaner. He was glad he didn't have to answer, and he quickly reached down and started picking up the strands of bulbs and tossing them into the box.

"That hurts!"
"What's he doing?"
"Ouch!"
Bobby's relatives moaned in unison.
"Is he crazy?" Bobby shouted.
And then dozens of bulbs came pouring into the box,
falling all around him.

The light stayed on the rest of the day. The closet
door remained open. Bobby heard the McGillicuddys as
they worked in other parts of the house. Every few
minutes, Mr. McGillicuddy would walk through the foyer
with his hands full of winter clothes, mumbling, "Why
do I have to take these clothes upstairs? I'll just be
bringing them down again in the fall."

Later, Bobby would see Mr. McGillicuddy, through
the open closet door, with his hands and arms full of
books, still talking to himself, "Why do I have to bring

all these books downstairs? I'll just be taking them upstairs in the summer."

At least Mr. McGillicuddy made Bobby laugh.

Only a few of the bulbs were in a position to see what was going on outside the open door. Besides Bobby there was Uncle Flicker, Dimmer, and Bobby's mom that had ended up where they could see.

While Mr. McGillicuddy continued his up and down trips with clothes and books, the bulbs watched in silence, except for Uncle Flicker who rambled on about how dumb Mr. McGillicuddy was for throwing the bulbs haphazardly into the box. Flicker was sure all of them were going to be thrown away.

Aunt Shining finally had enough. *"That's it, Flicker. We all know we are in trouble. You don't need to keep reminding us."*

Since Aunt Shining always had the last word with Uncle Flicker, that was the end of any more trash talk.

Every spring, Mrs. McGillicuddy ran the vacuum cleaner inside the closet. She would always ask Mr. McGillicuddy to set the boxes out in the foyer for her so she could properly clean. Normally, they remained there for a couple of days.

However, in late afternoon, after many trips up and down the stairs moving books and clothes and whatever else Mrs. McGillicuddy wanted moved, Mr. McGillicuddy decided he would clean the closet himself.

"Did you eat something to make you feel stronger, John?"

"What do you mean, dear?"

"You know very well what I mean."

"No, I really don't."

"Uh huh." Mrs. McGillicuddy didn't always wear her bifocals, but she had today. She peered over the top of them and looked at her husband. "When was the last time you ever volunteered to dust off those clothes and run the vacuum cleaner?"

Mr. McGillicuddy didn't have time to answer.

"You have never volunteered before," she said, "So why now?"

He remained silent.

"Well?"

"No real reason, Jane. I just was trying to help. I thought maybe we could finish everything today and this would make it quicker."

"Well, aren't you quite the wonderful husband, John McGillicuddy. I'll just take you up on that offer. Go clean the closet."

Mr. McGillicuddy was already on the way, tugging the vacuum cleaner along the floor.

Bobby watched over the edge of the box and saw Mr. McGillicuddy, who was whistling softly, shove the box to his right. Then he moved the vacuum to the opposite end of the long closet and clicked on the toe switch. VAAROOM.

The vacuum roared, and Bobby realized he had never been inside the closet when the vacuum cleaner was actually used. It was so loud that his ears hurt, and he hoped Mr. McGillicuddy would hurry and get finished.

He got his wish less than two minutes later when Mr. McGillicuddy turned off the vacuum cleaner, slid the box back into the middle of the closet, switched off the light, and slammed the door shut.

There was silence for only a few moments and then Bobby heard Aunt Shining. "*Just like that, spring-cleaning is over and we never even got out of this dungeon. It's not fair.*"

Bobby knew it wasn't fair, but what could they do? There would be months of darkness jammed inside a box with twisted bulbs, stacked in tangled clumps, and wrapped around each other.

He lay there for a few minutes, thinking how nice it would have been to spend two days in the hallway, when suddenly the door flew open.

The voice of Mrs. McGillicuddy blared loudly. At first, Bobby couldn't see her, but it was easy to hear her. In fact, he thought the neighbor next door might hear her.

"John, are you out of your mind?"

Before Mr. McGillicuddy could answer, she yelled, "You come here right now!"

Bobby listened, but didn't hear any footsteps. "Are you coming?"

Bobby heard footsteps running into the foyer.

"What is it, dear? Are you okay?"

"Don't play innocent with me, John. The door is shut, the vacuum cleaner is back in the pantry, and you are watching television."

"So?"

Bobby chuckled at the thought of Mr. McGillicuddy trying to sound like an innocent man.

"So, how did you get this done so quickly?"

"What do you mean, Jane?" He tried to sound brave.

"Did you really run the vacuum cleaner and dust the clothes?"

"I most certainly did," he said proudly.

Before she could continue her questioning, a noise came from the kitchen.

Ting! Ting! Ting!

"Oh, there's the oven timer. The roast is done. John, are you sure you cleaned this closet?" she asked, as she walked toward the kitchen.

"Of course I cleaned it." Mr. McGillicuddy sounded braver the farther she got away from him.

He waited until she was in the kitchen, and then he went into the closet and dragged the box to the doorway. "I guess I better try and get these things straightened out."

But before he could do anything, Mrs. McGillicuddy's voice rang out from the kitchen, "Come on, John, it's time to eat."

That was all Mr. McGillicuddy needed. "Guess I'll have to do this later tonight or tomorrow," he said.

Little did he know he would never get the chance.

3

The End of Spring-cleaning

The closet was dark, except for a thin ray of light shining under the door. It was barely visible to Bobby, as he lay squished against bulbs from his own family, and some of the other strands.

He remembered Mr. McGillicuddy's half-hearted rearrangement of the bulbs and how the box had never left the closet.

Yesterday, the closet door had been left open until mid afternoon, and Bobby had enjoyed a few rays of sunshine. He had seen the McGillicuddys pass by the door from time to time as they hurried to finish cleaning their house from top to bottom.

Mrs. McGillicuddy had reminded her husband many times that they must be finished before the predicted rainstorm arrived.

"I don't want you caught taking all that trash outside while it's raining and then tracking mud back into the house."

Bobby remembered Mr. McGillicuddy's mumbled reply. "The rain probably won't even get here, and I'll believe that prediction about possible tornados this weekend when I see one."

But at least this time the weatherman had been correct because Bobby could hear the noise of the raindrops hitting the roof, and they were getting louder and louder.

"Anybody else hear the rain?" Bobby asked, hoping to hear from someone in his family. *"Come on guys, let's talk. Somebody say something. We've got a long, lengthy wait ahead of us inside this closet."*

He had no idea how wrong he was.

4

First the Rain

As he listened to the rain pounding on the roof, Bobby heard a familiar voice. It came from only inches away, but he could not see her because two bulbs from a regular strand were squashed against her, blocking his view.

"What's happening, Bobby?"

"Is that you, Mom? Where are you?"

"I'm not sure, but I can't be far away. It's impossible to see. We've had all these other bulbs pressed up against us. I must have five different strands wrapped around me."

She sounded irritated and tired. Bobby said, "You sound like you are just below me. It's good to hear you."

"What's that noise, Bobby? Your dad wants to know too."

"I think it's the rain. Mrs. McGillicuddy said there is supposed to be a bad storm coming. Is Dad next to you?"

"Yes, but his face is right up against the side of the box."

"Can he talk?" Bobby asked.

"Not much. We've been fairly uncomfortable since Christmas, but now this is even worse after all those bulbs were thrown in here yesterday. Can you see your siblings?"

Before Bobby could answer, he heard the muffled voice of his dad.

"It will take a miracle to ever get this discombobulated chaos in order."

Bobby smiled. Good old Dad he thought. He loves to use big words.

"What's that word mean, Bobby?" It was his favorite cousin, Energizer.

"Oh, Daddy! You are so funny. You say the weirdest things. I mean like weird, Dad."

"Is that you, Ding-a-Ling?" Bobby whispered. That was Bobby's nickname for his sister, Sparkle, because he thought she always said the goofiest things.

"*Is Dad showing off again, big brother?*" It was his little brother, Dimmer, who didn't ever have very much to say and was one of just two tiny narrow blinking bulbs on the Bright family strand.

The other "blinker," as they liked to call themselves, was Bobby's other sister, quiet, little Twinkle. Even though she was shy, she did think of herself as a star. In fact, she had been named Twinkle because Bobby's mom and dad had thought she looked like a twinkling star. They had adopted both of them ten years ago on the very day the Bright family had received their magical powers during a conveyor belt accident at the Busy Lights and Bulbs Factory. A huge jolt of electricity had been injected into all of them, which was the reason they could speak "Bulbese."

Bobby and the other bulbs on the Bright family strand were regular oval-shaped indoor Christmas tree light bulbs. "*They are different from us but they will be in our family because they have our same magical powers.*"

Bobby still remembered his mom and dad's words when later that day the bulbs were boxed and shipped with thousands of other lights, to all parts of the world. Dimmer and Twinkle were a different size but they would always be members of the Bright family.

"Hi, guys," Bobby always loved to hear them talk. They spoke in a much higher pitch, which gave them a distinctly different "Bulbese" accent.

Twinkle provided the explanation. "We're both okay, Bobby. Even Mr. McGillicuddy's goofiness couldn't keep us apart. We are lucky because we don't have any bulbs twisted around us."

Boom! Boom! Boom!

The loud clap of thunder that shook the house interrupted the conversation. The sound of the rain pounding on the roof, and the wind became much louder. Then there was another loud Boom! Boom! Boom!

"What's happening?" Bobby heard Uncle Flicker from the edge of the box where he was hanging.

Before he could answer, Bobby heard another voice. It was his timid cousin, Blushing. "Is that rain I'm hearing, Bobby?"

Bobby could just barely see her because of the bulbs lying on top of him. However, there was no question she looked frightened.

And then, the noise they heard next gave all of them reason to be scared.

Vroom! Puhruush! Chug-chug-chug!

5

The Tornado Is Here

"**E**very channel is reporting tornados on the ground west and north of town. Piedmont and Yukon have baseball size hail, and I can hear it hitting our windows. I have never seen it this dark."

Bobby heard Mrs. McGillicuddy's voice outside the closet door.

"It's a giant tornado, John. I am so frightened. Mick Ritchell on channel fifty-five said it was the strongest he's ever seen. Should we go to the bedroom or here?"

"I think we better..."

Bobby didn't hear the rest of Mr. McGillicuddy's answer. The sound in the distance grew louder as it got closer.

Whoooosssssh! Baroom! Whoooossssh! Baroom! Whooooooosh!

He remembered hearing a similar sound a few years ago when the bulbs were in their usual spot at the back of the big Christmas tree in the huge room the McGillicuddys liked to call their Sports Arena. In the same room, the McGillicuddys were watching a movie on television.

Bobby had never "seen" a movie but he had heard voices and sounds from the television set in previous years.

The sound he now heard was the same sound he had heard then. It was the sound of what humans called a "train."

Bobby recalled Mr. McGillicuddy saying to Mrs. McGillicuddy, "John Wayne can do it all, Jane. He'll knock that guy off the train."

"And you'd like that, wouldn't you, Mr. John Wayne McGillicuddy."

Bobby didn't remember much more about that night except John Wayne was what humans called a big movie star and Mr. McGillicuddy loved being named after him.

"And you think you're a big star too?" Bobby remembered Mrs. McGillicuddy laughing after she said that.

But this was no laughing matter. The house was beginning to shake. The clothes in the closet swayed back and forth, and some of the hangers dropped to the floor. Tornado sirens were wailing in the distance, and that train noise was getting closer.

"*It's a tornado,*" Bobby shouted, and he remembered the McGillicuddys talking about what would happen when the whirling tornado prepared to veer downward from the sky, wreaking destruction with its long sweeping tail. People, buildings, and cars could be sucked into the air and destroyed in a matter of seconds.

"*I'm so terrified.*" It was Bobby's mom. "*The room is shaking. The box is shaking. We are all shaking. This is so scary.*"

Outside the closet came the voice of Mr. McGillicuddy, "It's a tornado, Honey. Get in the closet right now!"

"What about Rocket?"

"What did you say?" yelled Mr. McGillicuddy.

"I said, 'what about Rocket?' What are we going to do? Can't you hear him barking?"

"There's nothing we can do," Mr. McGillicuddy shouted back. He's in the garage and he's as safe there as anyplace. Now get in the closet."

Before Mrs. McGillicuddy could say another word, an incredible force of wind came tearing through the foyer, and there was the sound of breaking glass as the dining room window was ripped apart by the heavy wind.

The sound was deafening.

Currrusssh! Currussh! Currusssh!

The rush of wind forced the door open and it swung completely back against the wall. From near the top of the box, Bobby watched in horror. He heard the hinges creak and start to pull free from the doorframe.

He saw Mrs. McGillicuddy pushed inside the closet by Mr. McGillicuddy and, in that instant, one of the things that would change so much of Bobby's life happened.

Mrs. McGillicuddy brushed the side of the box and fell forward. She barely managed to keep her balance but was not able to keep from stepping on something. Even with the loud sound of wind and rain, she heard a "crunching" sound. A second later the force of the wind slammed the door shut.

Bobby heard the "crunching" sound just before he heard Mrs. McGillicuddy's loud voice.

"Find the light, John! I am petrified. Please turn the light on, Honey."

"I'm trying to reach the switch, but I'm stepping on bulbs." Bobby heard that same "crunching" sound just before Mr. McGillicuddy found the light switch and the closet was filled with light.

The first thing Mrs. McGillicuddy saw was the box with bulbs dangling down the sides and onto the floor. "I thought you told me you cleaned all this up. Look at this mess."

"Not now, Jane. A tornado is approaching and you're fussing about Christmas tree light bulbs."

Before he could say another word, the noise became even more deafening. Vuhroom! Puhroosh! Chug-Chug-Chug! Mrs. McGillicuddy screamed hysterically as the box was lifted off of the floor, and more bulbs spilled out.

And then, the noise became even louder.

"We can't stay, Jane. Get out of here. We've got to try and make it to the bedroom closet. Let's go."

The walls of the closet were shaking and suddenly the floor lifted upward. Up and down. Up and down. The pieces of parquet on the floor began to bend and stretch and pop loose.

Just like a roller coaster. Up and down. Up and down.

Mr. and Mrs. McGillicuddy pushed on the door together. The enormous pressure of the wind was so strong they couldn't make it move.

Then, a split second later, Whoosh! another powerful gust of wind sucked the door open.

The McGillicuddy's were lifted off of their feet and into the air. Bobby watched in horror as they were propelled from the closet, still clutching each other, crashed with tremendous force into the staircase railing, and fell to the floor.

Meanwhile, the rush of air pulled the remaining bulbs from the box. Bobby bounced on the floor as more pieces of parquet began to tear loose and sail toward the closet ceiling.

The door had been snapped open with such force that it banged off the wall and the hinges began to rip free from the doorframe.

The house shook, and at that moment, all of the bulbs were blown into the foyer.

Bobby watched fearfully as the rain gushed into the dining room through the shattered front window and the wind blew the rain into the foyer. He saw the bulbs begin to be covered with water as he stared in amazement at part of a tree limb.

Small pieces of tree branches floated between the foyer and the living room.

There was no question a giant tornado had struck the McGillicuddy's house. Even though very dangerous storms were part of Oklahoma's springtime weather, there had never been a tornado near the McGillicuddy's house during the ten years Bobby and his family had lived there.

There had been times when Bobby had heard the noise of loud wind, but never sounds this terrifying.

Whoooosh. Whoooosh.

Another huge rush of air blew through the broken dining room window and Bobby saw some of the other tangled and twisted bulbs fly through the air and land in a large puddle of water on the now soaked Persian rug.

In the garage, Rocket continued to bark as the noise became louder and louder.

Bobby was able to see his two sisters, brother, and mom and dad. They all looked frightened, and they had every reason to be.

And then, as if someone had turned off the sound on a loudspeaker system, the noise ended.

6

The Tornado Worsens

Once again, the sound became deafening. The front door ripped loose from the frame and bounced into the foyer.

Bobby would remember later, as he discussed the nightmare with his family, that their lives had been saved when they were lifted into the air for the third time.

The bulbs clanked against the wall before falling back to the floor. In that instant, they were ripped free from some of the other strands.

Many of those bulbs weren't so lucky. As they were blown into the rising water, they were crushed into tiny pieces by the McGillicuddy's beautiful German chandelier. It came crashing down from the ceiling, spraying sharp pieces of crystal throughout the room.

The broken chips spinning into the air looked like flakes of snow flying throughout the foyer.

Across the room, Mr. McGillicuddy lifted Mrs. McGillicuddy to her feet. She was shaking in his arms and crying as he tried to pull her from the foyer. But, he was too late.

Bobby watched in horror as the heavy front door, which had been ripped from the doorframe, spun like a discus in midair and slammed into Mrs. McGillicuddy, knocking her against the brick wall that separated the foyer from the living room.

The door shattered into many pieces and splinters of wood flew through the air, striking the neck, arms, and back of Mr. McGillicuddy. He fell forward, hit his head on the heavy wooden sideboard in front of the brick wall, and fell to the floor.

Sitting on top of the massive oak sideboard were three Frederick Remington sculptures, which the McGillicuddy's had owned for more than 25 years. The bronze art pieces were knocked to the floor and the one titled *Mountain Man* struck Mrs. McGillicuddy's right leg.

Bobby watched in disbelief as the water continued to rise around the McGillicuddys, who both lay motionless, just a few feet apart.

Bobby could see the severe damage the tornado had caused and he was sure that if they were to survive, the wind and rain would have to stop soon. He wished there was something he could do to make that happen. And then, almost like magic, his wish became true. It was suddenly very quiet.

Outside, the tornado's menacing twisting tail had disappeared into the sky.

It was as if the air had been sucked out of what was left of the foyer and the dining room.

The house quit shaking.

What seemed like many minutes of terrifying noise, wind, and rain, had actually been less than a minute.

Now that there was no wind and only a light rain still falling through the smashed dining room window, the water standing in the foyer began slowly rolling over the edge of the floor and into the McGillicuddy's sunken living room.

Bobby and the other bulbs in his family watched in silence. They were in shock. The realization of what had happened was the destruction in front of them. The front door was gone, the handrail on the staircase was cracked in half, and pictures lay on the floor floating in puddles of water.

The Bright family strand lay inches from the baseboard. Bobby looked across the room and his eyes were focused on the McGillicuddys, pinned beneath the large table. It was leaning sideways, one of its legs split in half, teetering from side to side and looking as if it would collapse to the floor at any moment.

Now, for the first time, he saw blood running from Mrs. McGillicuddy's right leg. He worried if she would be okay and if she and Mr. McGillicuddy would live through this horrible tornado. Even though he only saw them for a few hours each year, he felt as if the McGillicuddys were like a mom and dad to the whole Bright family.

But those thoughts were suddenly interrupted by the frightened voice of his real mom.

"Bobby!" she shrieked. "It's your father." When he turned his head, he immediately knew why his mom was so scared.

Bobby had a clear look at him. Dimmer, Twinkle and Sparkle could also see him. They all knew it was bad.

The top of his head was shattered. Bobby could see filaments from inside.

"Oh, no!" said Aunt Glaring, who sat in the pod at the end of the strand and next to Bobby.

Questions ricocheted throughout the strand.

"What's happening?"

"Is something wrong?"

"What's going on?"

"Is someone in trouble?"

Then the booming voice of Bobby's favorite uncle came from the very final pod at the opposite end. "Tell me right now, Bobby. What's the problem? Why is your mom crying?"

"It's Dad, Uncle Flicker. He's been crushed. The top of his head is open."

Cries of disbelief echoed through the strand.

Bobby looked straight ahead with a blank stare.

His mom pleaded, "Bobby. Please help him. Your daddy needs you. Please help him."

But it was his father's voice that brought Bobby back to reality.

"*Son, I can hear all of you. That may be good news. It's just that I feel very weak and what's left of my head is hurting.*

Bobby was only two pods away but could barely hear his father's slight whisper.

"*Dad, speak louder and tell me exactly how you feel.*"

"*I am speaking loudly, Bobby. I just feel very weak. My head is hurting.*"

"*What else, Dad? Try speaking louder.*"

"*I am speaking loudly,*" he repeated, but Bobby strained to hear the words.

"*Does anything else hurt?*" Bobby twisted forward and leaned around his mom so he could see his dad.

"*Not now, Bobby, I've got to sleep.*"

What Bobby saw made him quickly turn his head away. When he looked again, he saw small shards of glass barely hanging from his shattered top.

"*Please, Dad, try to tell me more.*" He waited, but there was no answer.

"*He's sleeping, Bobby,*" said his mom, and she started crying again.

Bobby and his mom cried together. Aunt Glaring joined them, as tears rolled down her cheeks.

Bobby had cried only one other time during the ten years since he and his family had been created by the conveyor belt accident.

But now, he definitely had a reason. He was frightened because he knew it would probably take stronger magical powers than he possessed to save his dad.

His thoughts about his dad were interrupted when he heard a moan from Mr. McGillicuddy, who was near the fallen sideboard across the room. He appeared to be regaining consciousness, although he was still face down and pinned to the floor by the thick wooden leg of the table. Bobby watched him raise his head and attempt to turn his body.

"Oh my Gosh!" His voice shattered the silence in the foyer, as he twisted himself onto his side. For the first time he saw his wife's body lying behind him and to his left.

He saw the huge sculpture lying against her and he could see some blood on the back of the calf of her right leg.

"Jane, Jane. Jane, answer me! Please, Honey, say something!"

But there was no answer.

His whole body began to shake. The crying got louder. Intermixed with the tears and the wailing was his plea for help. "Can anyone hear me? Help us! Help us!"

Even with the front door blown away, and the dining room window shattered, there was no one who could hear his voice. There certainly weren't any neighbors brave enough yet to go outside and check on the destruction.

"Help me! Help my wife!" Then he shouted even louder, "Someone, please come help us!"

But there were no voices in the distance and no patter of feet racing up the driveway. There was only silence.

Mr. McGillicuddy shouted one more time, and then, after glancing at his wife, rolled over onto the floor and passed out again.

It was silent, except for the sound of Rocket whimpering in the garage.

Mr. McGillicuddy would not learn, until much later, that no one heard his cries for help, and, it would take him some time before he would ever admit that some very strange things happened.

But had they not, the McGillicuddys would have never spent another day together again.

7

Let The Heroics Begin

B obby turned to his mom. *"Look at Mrs. McGillicuddy. Can you* see her?"

"Yes, just barely. Some of those bulbs in the middle of that rug are blocking part of my view."

"Blood is all over her leg, Mom. She and Mr. McGillicuddy are unconscious."

"Oh my! Bobby you've got to do something."

He started to answer, but his mom kept talking.

"What am I talking about? Just listen to me! Your father's head is broken. He will never be able to shine again. We are lying in the middle of a disaster, and most likely will be thrown away."

"Well, what do we do, Mom?"

"What do you mean? What do WE do? WE don't do anything, because WE can't do anything." Her voice was gruff. Bobby was taken aback. She didn't sound normal.

"What's wrong with you?"

"Nothing is wrong, Bobby. Just because WE can't do anything, doesn't mean YOU can't do something. YOU are going to make it right."

"What are you talking about?"

"What I'm talking about is this. You are special. You are different. We can cheer. We can encourage you. We can maybe help a little. But Bobby Bright, it is you who must, and can, save Mrs. McGillicuddy, and hopefully all of us. Now go do it, my son, and we will cheer for you."

A few pods to the right, Bobby's cousin Blushing said, "You can do it, Bobby."

Three pods away were his brother and two sisters. They leaned to their left, across their parents, and clinked him on the top of his head.

The magic of his family around him made Bobby feel better, and he wanted even more to save his father and Mrs. McGillicuddy. But, the question remained, how could he do it?

As the bulbs on the strand, soaked in water and still frightened, realized what Bobby must do, they joined in a loud cheer.

Bobby listened and the cheers helped him form an idea in his mind.

Moments after the cheers had stopped, Bobby heard a siren in the distance.

He could see the outer glass door only a few feet away. The glass was gone, except for a few shattered pieces, which hung precariously to the inner frame.

Tree limbs were scattered in the driveway. A huge trashcan was on its side near the small brick porch in front of the door.

It was amazing that the eight-foot tall wooden door had been propelled through the foyer like a tiny piece of paper, and yet the outer door still stood intact.

"Listen up, everyone," Bobby shouted, *"The only way to save her is to stop the bleeding."*

From the far end of the strand, Uncle Flicker's big voice boomed, *"What do you need me to do, Bobby?"*

"I've got a plan and you are a big part of it, Uncle Flicker."

"Tell me if you can see Mrs. McGillicuddy's leg. You are a lot closer to her." Bobby raised his voice so he

could be heard over the sirens. There was more than one emergency vehicle approaching.

"I can see a leg, nephew. It is not a pretty sight. There is a very deep gash."

Just then, Bobby saw through the glass door a huge red fire engine slowly turn the corner. It was followed by an ambulance, which also passed in front of the house. Seconds later, the sirens abruptly stopped.

Bobby heard doors opening, and men were shouting instructions to each other. He yelled to Uncle Flicker. "What did you just say?"

"I said, it is not a pretty sight. There is a very deep gash."

Before Bobby could continue, his mom interrupted. "What are those men saying, Bobby? Can you understand?"

"Not now, Mom."

"But do you think they can help us?"

"I don't know, Mom. Let me do what I have to do."

Then Bobby realized that maybe his mom was right. He listened for a moment, but the only human words he heard were more shouted instructions among the firemen. He heard one of them clearly say, "It's the second house, not the one on the corner. That's where the call came from." Bobby knew then, the McGillicuddy's corner house was not the one the emergency workers were interested in.

If no one was coming to help, he had to do something immediately.

"*We've got to stop the bleeding. That's the only way she will live.*" He raised his voice even louder so everyone could hear.

"*What do you mean when you say 'we', cousin?*" It was Energizer.

"*That's exactly what I mean. We are going to do it. It will take everyone if my plan is to work. For sure it is going to take you, Uncle Flicker, and Aunt Shining, and you too Blinker.*"

"Me? You've got to be kidding," Blinker said. "Nobody ever talks to me except my mom and dad. Why would anybody need me?"

"Well, I need you and Mrs. McGillicuddy definitely needs you. In fact, she needs all of us, so listen up!"

Aunt Shining looked over the top of her bifocals, as she asked her husband, *"Does he really believe that will work?"*

"I guess he does, dear. You remember last year when he flew through the air, right over the top of us, and shorted out the wall plug. If he hadn't, we would all be long gone, dead in a landfill some place."

"It sounds so frightening, Flicker."

"Well, you won't have time to think about it. If that woman is going to be saved it has to happen right now."

And then Bobby rolled up in front of both of them. He had spun himself free from his pod at the opposite end of the strand, and then rolled along the wet carpet to reach the other end.

"Do you understand my plan?"

"Yes, Nephew, but how are you going to manage lifting us in the air?"

"Just watch, but right now, just listen. You three have the toughest chore."

"What can I do, Bobby?"

"Blinker, don't panic, and don't whine. Just do what I tell you."

Bobby then turned to his uncle, "Okay. You remember me teaching you how to roll. You've got to do it inside the pod."

"Now everyone else, listen!" Bobby yelled down the strand. "You have to do what you did last year, when we all twisted together and tightened up in our pods. This time twist and try to roll at the same time. We have to move this strand across the room, and we have to do it quickly. Mrs. McGillicuddy's leg looks very bad." Then Bobby shouted, "Do it! Do it now!"

He watched and saw the strand move only a few inches as the bulbs twisted and tried to roll simultaneously. "Do it again!"

"I can't do this, Bobby." It was his cousin Dazzling.

"You better do it, Dazzling, or you won't be dazzling to anyone again."

"Is that a threat?" she huffed.

"No, it is fact. Do it! All of you!"

Bobby hated to be so forceful, but Mrs. McGillicuddy's life was hanging in the balance.

As the bulbs twisted and groaned, and the strand moved only a few more inches, Bobby yelled "Puhrumba" twice.

Then he launched himself into the air, and flew toward the wall socket that was only two feet from the broken table lying on Mr. and Mrs. McGillicuddy.

The bulbs stopped twisting. They watched in awe, just as they had done last December, when Bobby's family had been saved by his magical powers.

Some of the bulbs lost sight of him as he disappeared around the corner. "*Where is he, where did he go?*" asked his sister, Twinkle.

"*I can see him,*" shouted Flicker. "*He's circling near the wall socket. Now he's spinning in mid-air and looking at the two plugs.*"

"*What in the world is he doing that for?*" asked Flash.

"*He is checking out the wall socket and figuring out how we can get the plug into it.*"

"*This will never happen,*" Flash said pessimistically.

"*Puhrumba! Puhrumba! Puhrumba!*" The room vibrated with the sound of Bobby's voice as he shouted his magical words again and then dropped on to the floor.

"*Don't ever say the word 'never,' Flash. This is going to work.*"

He rolled as fast as he could toward his mom and, as he reached her, he noticed his dad was awake. He didn't look good with the top of his head gone, but he was smiling.

Before Bobby could say anything, his dad winked. "*Go get them, Son. Whether I make it or not doesn't matter now. Just do what you have to do.*"

It was then Bobby realized what his dad was saying. When bulbs are broken, they can no longer light. His dad would not be able to shine again. In fact, he might explode when the strand was plugged in, and lighting the bulbs was the whole key to his plan to save Mrs. McGillicuddy.

Time was running out.

"*No, Dad. I can't do this. If you are turned on, you will die.*"

"*Maybe not, Bobby. We don't know for sure.*"

"*But we can't take the chance, Dad.*"

"*Oh, yes we can, Bobby my boy. You do it. I love you. If I make it, we'll have lots to talk about. If not, I will have done my part to help save someone else.*"

"*No! You can't do this to your father!*" Bobby's mom was crying again.

"*Mom! Stop it!*"

"*He's right. Please, stop it,*" said his dad. "*No more arguments. Just do it!*"

And with those words ringing in his ears, Bobby rolled toward the other end where Uncle Flicker, Aunt Shining, and a trembling cousin Blinker waited. He wished he could do all of this by himself, pick up the plug, lift it in the air, fly to the wall socket and jam the plug into the two-prong outlet.

But as magical as Bobby was, he could not do this alone. He needed help and every bit of energy he could possibly muster, if they had a chance to save Mrs. McGillicuddy.

"Are you sure this will work?" Aunt Shining trembled.

"Won't know until we do it, will we?'" Bobby tried to sound nonchalant. It helped, since he was as frightened as every other bulb.

He was lying right beneath the wounded leg of Mrs. McGillicuddy. The bulbs on the strand had twisted and turned, and rolled, and tugged at each other the best that they could.

It had been marvelous, Bobby thought, seeing everyone working together. They had actually moved almost
five or six feet across the floor. For a human, that would
have been like driving a hundred miles on a trip.

Now it was time to do what had to be done.

"Listen up, everyone! Final instructions. This is the
hardest part."

"Harder than rolling across the floor? You got to be
kidding me."

"Be quiet, Bingo. When I fly into the air, and you see
me nose-diving toward the wall socket, be ready. You
know what will happen when I push the plug in. You will
feel that familiar surge of heat race through you. Here
we go everybody. Let's do it!"

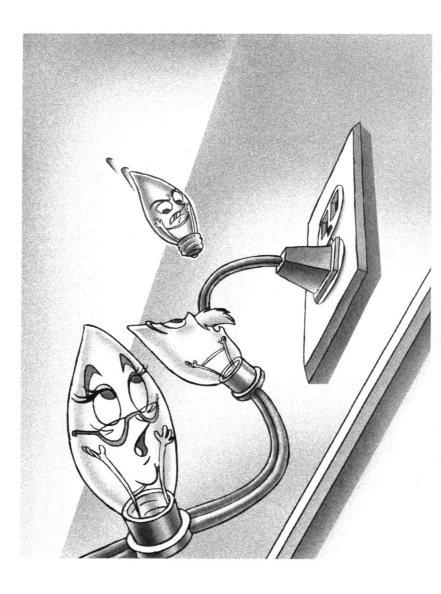

8
Completing the Plan

"**P**uhrumba! Puhrumba! Puhrumba!" Bobby shot into the air, and the two prongs of the plug in front of him looked like missiles on the bottom of a jet fighter.

"*Zerplonk! Zerplonk! Zerplonk!*"

He swept upward from the ground and turned in a wide arc.

"*Amazing!*" his cousins Whitening, Bingo, and Sparkling shouted in unison as they watched from the floor.

There was a collective gasp as the bulbs were pulled into the air.

"*Let's go, my favorite nephew!*" There was no fear in the booming voice of Uncle Flicker. He had the best seat, or the worst seat, depending on how a bulb felt about being launched six feet upward into the air.

Next to him, holding on to her bifocals, with her eyes wide open was Aunt Shining. Only rushes of air came from her mouth. She was too frightened to say anything, but she remembered in that very instant what had happened only a few seconds earlier, before they had magically flown into the air.

At the very bottom of the curled up bulbs, Bobby caught sight of his mom and dad. Even from six feet in the air, he saw the dazed look on their faces.

His attention quickly turned to the challenge. He steered the plug into a high arch, which looked like the top of a question mark, and then began to turn downward.

No more talking, no more plans. It was time.

"This is it, everyone!" He yelled as loudly as he could, and then, with his bottom squarely against the back of the plug, and leaning forward so he could see, he nose-dived toward the wall.

In the distance, he could see the two slits in the wall socket.

His speed increased. He knew he must not miss. If the two prongs didn't connect, he would not have enough energy to do all of this again.

"It's time for all of us to work together. Lean forward and give me as much pressure as you can when

we hit the socket." Then, he spoke as loud as he could, "Here we go!"

Loud thrills of delight echoed through the strand.

"Way to go, Bobby."

"We did it!"

"Yippee!"

"You did it, Bobby."

"No, all of you helped do it," Bobby yelled.

"Can you believe that, Shining?" Uncle Flicker had a grin that was even wider than his handlebar mustache.

"He did it! The boy did it!"

"On the first try," his aunt said, in a voice that still quivered from the fear she had experienced just seconds earlier.

"The plug is in the wall. I can feel the heat starting to come back into my body. Oh it feels good."

Aunt Shining's words were interrupted by Bobby's shouted orders.

"We're not done yet."

His plan was working, but it wasn't complete. *"You've done a good job, but not all of the bulbs are up against Mrs. McGillicuddy."*

The bulbs needed to be very tightly coiled together and covering the large gash on the calf of her leg if they were to provide enough pressure on the wound to stop the bleeding. Only then would there be a chance.

Many of the bulbs had been lifted into the air when the plug struck the wall socket. When they fell backward, they landed close to, or on top of Mrs. McGillicuddy. However, those bulbs on the floor that didn't make it airborne were not up against her yet.

However, they were managing with great effort to get closer. Each wanted to be a part of saving Mrs. McGillicuddy.

Only Dazzling griped. *"I can't believe I'm lying in this gooey mess. What will it do to me?"*

Bobby frowned and replied, *"Just be quiet, miss prim and proper. Don't say another word."*

He looked to the other end of the strand where the remaining bulbs were twisting, turning, and spinning onto Mrs. McGillicuddy. It was then he saw his dad, who was still alive, and, for just a moment, Bobby swore he saw just a flicker of light from the top of his head.

As much as he wanted to take time to roll over to him and hug him, he couldn't. There were still things to do, and he was beginning to feel weaker. His strength had diminished after the rapid downward flight, where in the last split second he had thought he was going to miss the two slits in the wall socket. However, he had managed to turn at the last moment, and he miraculously drove the prongs inward.

When they locked into the socket he was jarred badly, chipping the right side of his bulb case. He was sore from the collision, but there was no time to worry about that right now.

"You have to be tighter against the wound," he shouted.

"If I was any closer, I'd be inside it," screamed Uncle Glimmer. He was covered with water and specks of blood. He had landed directly on top of the cut on her leg.

"No wonder, I'm in pod number 13. Part of being unlucky."

"Depends on how you look at it, Uncle," Bobby answered. "You are doing more than anyone. If the flow of blood stops, you will be a major reason. Are you getting hot?"

"Oh, yeah. I'm warming up. I'm much hotter now."
And so were the other bulbs.

"Now, we must keep her warm, but most importantly we need to keep the pressure on the wound to stop the bleeding," Bobby reminded all of the bulbs. Then, he added, "Shine like you did for Remington last Christmas everyone."

"Shouldn't you be getting back here to your pod, Bobby?"

"I'm coming, Mom."

One weak "Puhrumba!" was all he could manage, but it was enough to allow him to glide to his pod, where he screwed himself in and waited.

He began to feel warmer, and he knew that if that was happening to him, then it was also happening to the other 24 bulbs. If they could remain tightly packed against her, there still might be hope for Mrs. McGillicuddy.

"It's stopped!" The cry from Uncle Glimmer came three minutes later.

"*The wound in her leg is starting to dry.*"

"*Oh, I wish I could be there,*" Flicker's voice boomed from the floor just beneath the wall socket. He, Shining, and Blinker had played a major role in the success of the plug being jammed into the socket. But they were too far away to provide any heat against Mrs. McGillicuddy's body. All of the other bulbs were either touching her body, or like most, partially wrapped around the wound.

Uncle Flicker started to say something else when Bobby interrupted with a loud "*SSHHH!*"

There was movement from Mr. McGillicuddy, who had remained motionless and unconscious during all of the bulbs' work to save Mrs. McGillicuddy. He turned onto his side and rose up on an elbow. He had a large cut across the top of his head and there was dried blood on his cheek

He took one look at his wife, and remembered immediately what he saw before passing out ten minutes earlier.

"Jane!" He yelled loudly. "Can you hear me, Darling?"

He stared at her as if he was in a trance. He waited, but there was no answer.

"*What's he saying, Bobby?*" asked his dad.

"*He's asking if she can hear him,*" Bobby answered.

"Please talk to me, say something," but there was no answer.

Then Mr. McGillicuddy managed to get to his knees. He could see his wife clearly.

He remembered seeing her not moving and lying face down before he had passed out. He remembered the sight of blood and a bad cut on her leg. But now, he realized that he was looking at Christmas tree light bulbs lying in a circle on top of the calf on her right leg. But even more amazing, the bulbs were shining brightly.

He shook his head. He closed his eyes, and slowly opened them. The bulbs were still there.

"My God above! What is happening here?" he shouted.

And then, almost like destiny, the sound of a voice came from outside the open dining room window.

It was the beginning of the answer to his question.

"Is anyone in there? This is the fire department."

9

It was a Miracle

A fireman opened what was left of the front door. He saw Mrs. McGillicuddy lying on the floor. Two more firefighters followed, and all three saw Mr. McGillicuddy staring at them.

"Sir, are you all right?" the first firefighter asked. There was no answer.

"Sir, we are here to help you. Is this your wife?"

Mr. McGillicuddy looked straight ahead and said nothing.

"Christopher, tell that paramedic to call for another ambulance right now." The last fireman turned around, and went back outside. One of the firemen bent down to check on Mrs. McGillicuddy while the other one stepped into the living room. "There's a lot of blood on the floor in here, David," he shouted back to the other fireman who was examining Mrs. McGillicuddy.

"Oh my gosh, come back in here Scott, I just found the problem. There aren't any cuts or damage to her head, but will you look at this?"

David returned to the room. "What is it?"

"Look here at this," he said and pointed to the Christmas tree light bulbs tightly packed against her leg.

"There's the blood," he said, as he gently moved the bulbs off the wound in Mrs. McGillicuddy's leg.

"I just felt for her pulse and she's got a weak one." He turned to Mr. McGillicuddy, "Sir, can you tell me anything about what happened? Did you see your wife get injured?"

Mr. McGillicuddy started to mumble an answer but was interrupted when the glass door opened and two paramedics raced into the room. One of them yelled to the fireman named Christopher, "Scoot all those Christmas lights out of the way. What are they doing here anyway?"

With a quick kick from his mud soaked boots, Christopher moved three strands lying in the middle of the foyer against the wall.

"Look at these lights," yelled one of the paramedics. "What happened here? Why would Christmas tree lights be plugged into a wall socket during a tornado?"

"That's just what I was getting ready to tell you," the fireman named David answered. "Look at these bulbs. It's like somebody intentionally placed them here."

The paramedic touched them. "Ouch!" he shrieked. "Those little guys are hot."

"You bet we are," Bobby said

"What's he saying, Son?"

Bobby laughed, and whispered to his dad, "They just figured out we are hot, but they don't understand how we got plugged in and shining during a tornado."

"Have they mentioned anything about Mrs. McGillicuddy?"

Bobby didn't answer because he saw two more firemen in the dining room. They had just entered the house by walking through the hole in the dining room wall, where once there had been a window.

Then Bobby saw the hand of one of the paramedics, and suddenly he and his family were shoved off of Mrs. McGillicuddy's leg.

"Look at this, Lance," said the other medical worker named Sharpie, who bent down to get a closer look at Mrs. McGillicuddy's leg.

"We've got to get her out of here. Her pulse is extremely low."

"Unplug these bulbs," shouted one of the other firemen.

"Don't you touch those bulbs!" said Mr. McGillicuddy, as he suddenly jumped to his feet. He had not moved from the kneeling position the firemen and medics had found him in until now. He stood in front of them with a crazy look on his face.

"They saved her," he screamed. "Don't you understand? They saved her life. Don't unplug them. Don't hurt them."

One of the fireman grabbed Mr. McGillicuddy. "Calm down, sir! You'll be fine."

"For goodness' sake! Get her to a hospital," Mr. McGillicuddy yelled, as a fireman pulled him out of the way, "and be careful with those bulbs."

At that moment, a third medical worker rushed into the room pushing a stretcher on wheels.

The paramedic named Lance swept the bulbs out of the way and yelled to him, "Get over here quickly, Rocky."

"You bet," he squealed. "I was just getting there."

"What are they doing?"

"Ouch!"

"That hurts!"

"Ugh! I just hit the wall." The shouts in Bulbese echoed throughout the strand as it was kicked away from Mrs. McGillicuddy, and like a twisting snake, slid across the floor of the foyer toward the bedroom hallway.

"I'm going to have whiplash," yelled Uncle Flicker, as he and Aunt Shining, who were at the end of the strand, were snapped up and down, when the plug was partially pulled loose from the wall socket and the lights went dark.

Mr. McGillicuddy ranted and raved, "What are you doing? Be careful with those bulbs. They saved her! They saved her! Don't you see what they did?"

"He's in shock, Scott. Take him outside."

The firemen grabbed him by the arm. "Come on, sir. They are ready to move your wife to the ambulance."

It was as if those were the words he needed to hear. "She's alive," he shouted. "She's alive! Is she going to be okay?"

"We'll know in a few minutes, sir," one of the paramedics said, as she was wheeled through the doorway and quickly loaded into the ambulance.

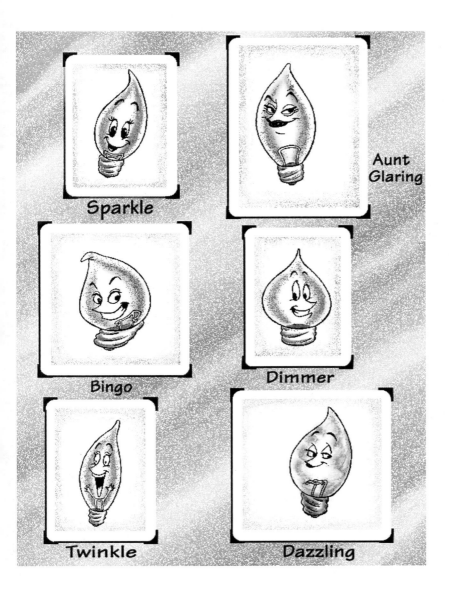

Sparkle

Aunt Glaring

Bingo

Dimmer

Twinkle

Dazzling

PART TWO

10

Mr. McGillicuddy Comes Home

A huge sheet of plastic fluttered in the light spring breeze where once there was a dining room window. Behind the plastic was a large sheet of plywood covering the opening.

To the left and in the middle of the front of the house, the outer glass door at the entrance still stood in place. Shards of glass, that had survived the tornado, hung in small pieces and occasionally blew from side to side whenever the wind would gust.

Behind the door was a massive eight foot tall piece of plywood that blocked anyone from entering the home.

It was 9 o'clock in the morning when the taxi pulled into the driveway. Mr. McGillicuddy got out of the back seat, reached inside the front window, and paid the driver. He stood there looking at his house and shaking his head as the taxi pulled away.

He had ridden in the ambulance to the hospital with Mrs. McGillicuddy two days ago. This was his first time home since her operation. He was tired, even though he had slept in her hospital room both nights. It was difficult, because his wife had awakened numerous times. She was still in pain, even with the medication, and because of her bruised right hip, she could not lie on her side. She was required to sleep on her back and remain very still. The lower part of her right leg was also elevated, placed in a sling that hung down from a bar above the bed.

Earlier this morning, they both were awake by six o'clock. She had convinced him she needed to be alone so she could get more sleep. The doctors agreed. They thought that with more rest and quiet she would probably have enough strength to return home in about three days.

Mr. McGillicuddy had obliged their wishes. Now, he stood alone in the driveway, staring at his house.

As bad as the front of the house appeared, Mr. McGillicuddy knew the neighbors next door, and two other houses farther down the street, had suffered much worse damage.

However, Phyllisjean's house, directly across the street, looked the same as it had before the tornado. Not one bit of damage, and, in fact, with all the rain during the storm, the grass was beginning to show some tinges of green.

He mumbled to himself, "I'm not looking forward to getting all of this fixed, but I better at least get started before Jane comes home."

With that thought in mind he hit the code on the garage door opener pad, and the overhead door creaked open.

Bobby was the first to speak. "*Someone is coming into the garage.*"

He expected the door from the garage into the kitchen hallway to open at any moment, and that's exactly what happened.

He saw Mr. McGillicuddy push the door slowly open and peer into the wrecked house.

Bobby could barely see him from his position near the end of the strand which stretched from the wall socket into the bedroom hallway. Uncle Flicker, Aunt Shining, and Blinker had a better view of the door because they were nearest the wall socket in the foyer, at the opposite end of the strand. However, Bobby was still able to see Mr. McGillicuddy's face and his confused expression.

"I can't believe this has happened," Mr. McGillicuddy said. He stood quietly and looked at the debris in the dining room. He walked to the wall and looked at a watercolor painting of two ladies in wide brimmed hats and long skirts sitting beneath a tree in a park, having a picnic on a blanket covered with plates, silverware, and food.

"It's ruined. Just look at it. Soaked. There's no chance to save it. Jane always loved that painting," he said quietly. Then he reached up, pulled the picture free from the two hooks, turned, and carried it out the door into the garage.

When he came back inside, he saw three strands of broken bulbs on the floor in the foyer, beneath the staircase handrail.

He bent down and picked through them. "These are headed to the dumpster. Most of them are broken. I'll just get some new ones at Christmas time." With that, he scooped the strands into his arms and walked out of the house.

"Are we in trouble?" asked Bobby's sister, Sparkle.

"I don't know. We could be."

"What do you mean?" Uncle Glimmer asked.

"Who knows what is going through his mind with all that's happened? But if he has already thrown out those other three strands, he might decide we're not needed either."

"No!" Aunt Shining cried. "This can't happen. We saved his wife's life. Doesn't he know that?"

"Calm down, Aunt Shining. We are not broken and smashed like those other bulbs. I think we are probably safe."

As soon as the words came out of his mouth, he realized he was wrong. But before he could say anything, his dad said, *"Don't start worrying because I'm broken. Think positively. I'm only one bulb. We look fine except for me. Plus, Flicker, you can see the closet from where you are. Aren't there some strands just outside of it that weren't damaged?"*

There was a pause and then Flicker answered. *"Yep. I'm looking at them. The ones I see look okay from here."*

"Then let's…" the words of Bobby's dad were interrupted by the telephone ringing in the kitchen, and Mr. McGillicuddy hurrying inside to answer it.

"Hello."

Mr. McGillicuddy held the receiver to his ear with his left hand while he reached over with his other hand and pulled a chair up to the desk.

"Yes, I just arrived 15 minutes ago."

He sat down in the small breakfast room next to the kitchen.

"I know I could have called you, Stan, but it was early, and it's Saturday morning. Besides, it wasn't that big of a deal getting the taxi."

Mr. McGillicuddy listened to his brother-in-law, but his eyes were focused on the kitchen. He was thoroughly amazed that there was no damage in the room, or in the kitchenette where he was sitting. And when he stared through the open gap window separating the kitchenette and the large recreation room, he could see no damage on the other side either.

With his attention on the kitchen area, he realized he had failed to answer his brother-in-law.

"She's doing better," he said, and then gave a report on Mrs. McGillicuddy's injuries. When he was finished, Stan had another question for him. Mr. McGillicuddy listened, and then answered, "Yes, I spoke with two of the doctors this morning, right after they had checked on her at 6:30."

As he listened to another question from Stan, Mr. McGillicuddy stood up, cupped the phone receiver under his chin, and balanced it on his left shoulder. He attempted to lean across from the desk and reach down and pick up some towels that were lying on the floor.

A light jingle reverberated from the kitchen.
Clank

"What was that, Bobby?"

"Sounded like Mr. McGillicuddy may have dropped the phone," Bobby said.

"Oh, that man is so clumsy," said his mom.

"Sorry, Stan. I was trying to pick up some towels. They were blown off the counter during the tornado."

Mr. McGillicuddy sat back down in the chair in the breakfast nook and answered another question from his brother-in-law.

"Yeah, I knew you did. You told me yesterday at the hospital you had driven by. I mean, you could have come into the house and looked around at the damage. That's the reason we gave you the key. I suppose the workers I called had already boarded everything up by the time you were here."

Mr. McGillicuddy scratched his nose and listened as Stan told him about many of their relatives calling to check on Jane. Mr. McGillicuddy tried to pay attention but his thoughts wandered back to the moment after the tornado when he had regained consciousness.

What happened while I was passed out? I remember rolling over and seeing her lying face down on the floor and the blood pouring from her leg. I thought she was dead. And then I came out of shock; at least that's what the paramedics told me. There she was, barely alive, but no longer bleeding. Then I got all those questions from the medical guys, and that fireman who rode in the ambulance with us. I mean, how could I explain it? And why did they think I was hiding something? I mean, did they actually think we sat around during tornadoes, and plugged in Christmas tree lights in case the electricity went out. Whose idea was that? And, how did the strand of bulbs get plugged into a wall socket? And, how did the bulbs end up packed against her leg so tightly that the pressure probably helped stop the bleeding and saved her life?

"What? Why are you yelling at me?"

He stood up and pushed the chair back from the small built-in desk and switched the phone receiver to his other ear.

"I'm sorry. I was listening to you, but I sort of started daydreaming about those Christmas bulbs I told you about. Stan, you know I believe in God," he continued, "And I believe in miracles, and this was some kind of a special miracle. But, how did it happen? I know you didn't see it, but it was amazing. Those bulbs are still lying right where they were when we left the house. I saw them a moment ago. I'm saving them forever. I'll tell you, Stan, it's eerie the more you think about it."

Then, Mr. McGillicuddy heard a click on the telephone line.

"Hey, Stan, I've got another call coming in. Let me call you later after I get some work done. I'm going to go buy a front door and a new window at Lowe's and try to have it fixed by the time Jane gets home in a few days."

He started to switch lines, but then said, "Why are you laughing?"

He listened to his brother-in-law, and then shouted, "Don't be so sarcastic. You just watch, I can fix those things myself. I'm not going to spend all of the insurance money on having other people come in to repair the door, window, and the stairwell. So, you go ahead and laugh at me if you want, but I'll get it done."

And with that, he clicked the button and switched to the other line where he heard his sister say, "Hello."

"Hi, Stephanie. Yeah, she is better."

Bobby let out a loud, "*Yippee!*" which got everyone's attention before he told them the great news.

"*Number one, guys, we have saved Mrs. McGillicuddy. Everyone should be proud. This wasn't one bulb doing it; this was each of us doing our part to apply pressure and stop the bleeding.*"

"*What else, Bobby?*"

"*Well, Sparkling,*" he said to his beautiful green cousin, "*Obviously the fact we saved Mrs. McGillicuddy* is wonderful, but she did suffer. She has a bruised hip and her injured leg is apparently in some kind of a cast or something that keeps it hanging in the air. I don't really understand that."

"When will she be home?" Aunt Glaring asked.

Twinkle chimed in too. "Yes, Bobby, when will she be home from the hospital?"

"Give me a chance to talk," he said. "Mr. McGillicuddy says she will be released in a few days, but there is even better news. Mr. McGillicuddy said there was no way our strand of bulbs would be thrown out. He sounded very serious. I think we are safe."

Mr. McGillicuddy made scrambled eggs and buttered some toast. He ate quickly, and wasn't really satisfied, but decided he could wait at least a couple of hours before it was time for lunch. He wasted no time in going to the garage, getting a measuring tape, and heading to the front door.

On the way, he stopped as he was passing the strand of lights plugged into the wall socket. He bent over and dropped to one knee to look at the bulbs that were closest to the wall. He leaned in closely and stared at the plug for a moment. It was slightly pulled loose from the socket. He shook his head, smiled, and said, "You bulbs are very, very special little fellas."

11

The Cleanup Begins

Mr. McGillicuddy was not happy about having to pick up a van at Lowe's Home Improvement Warehouse. However, it was the only way he could get started repairing the house immediately because the giant hardware store was not taking delivery or installation appointments until three weeks from now.

"No way am I going to wait that long." He was mumbling to himself as he walked into the dining room and began gathering up broken pieces of glass, small tree limbs, and leaves that had blown through the dining room window. It wouldn't take long to fill up the waist high blue container bin that he had brought inside the house.

He expected it would be a couple of hours before the rental van would be available.

Mr. McGillicuddy wanted to have the house as normal as possible by the time Mrs. McGillicuddy came home from the hospital. Many things would have to come later, like painting the staircase and the walls in the foyer. And there would definitely have to be a new floor in the foyer, plus new wallpaper in the dining room. But for now, he could put up a new front door and dining room windows. That would make her feel better when she arrived home.

As he continued to pick up the small branches and leaves in the dining room, he thought again how lucky she was to be alive and how fortunate he was that he had suffered only bruised ribs from the flying debris during the tornado. The emergency room doctor had suggested a deep heating gel that would reduce the pain. He planned to buy some at the pharmacy before picking up the van.

That happened sooner than expected when he got a phone call from Lowe's.

"How long are we going to have to lie here?"

"I don't know, Dazzling. I wasn't able to ask Mr. McGillicuddy before he left."

"Good line, Bobby." It was his cousin, Bingo.

Every bulb on the strand laughed as soon as he said it.

"I see nothing funny about that. Why are all of you laughing?"

"Because it's funny, Dazzling," said Uncle Glimmer.

"I won't call you Robert, if you won't make fun of me, Bobby."

"Whatever, Dazzling."

"So, Bobby," it was Energizer, "How long are we going to have to lie here?" All the bulbs chuckled again.

After a brief pause, another voice came from the middle of the strand, "So, Bobby, how long are we going to lie here?" But this time no one laughed.

"Poor Blinker," Bobby leaned over and whispered to his mom, "he just isn't funny, even if he says the same thing everyone else said."

"He tries," she said.

"I know, Mom."

"Well, you be nice to him and don't make fun of him."

Bobby started to reply but was interrupted by the sound of the garage door opening. Mr. McGillicuddy was back and ready to go to work.

Mr. McGillicuddy backed the rental van into the garage.

Before going to pick up the van, he had moved the dining room chairs into the living room. Also, with a lot of difficulty, he managed to move the serving buffet around the corner and partially into the foyer.

He had covered the dining room table with blankets and sheets, although he wasn't sure it was necessary. The table had so much water damage from the storm; it probably would be moved to a growing pile of trash and debris gathering at the front curb.

He opened the door and began to bring materials from the garage into the dining room. First, he brought in an armful of packages filled with bolts, screws, and nuts for putting the window frames together.

Then he made four trips to bring window frames into the house. The routine was the same each time. He would carefully take a step up from the garage into the hallway, gently place the frame on the floor, and then stand it upright. Once he got another grip on it, when he had it tightly clamped with both hands, he would slowly walk it into the dining room. The first two trips, he put the frames against the wall nearest the foyer. The third time, he leaned the frame against the table.

He felt just fine. He had picked up the truck an hour late, but other than that, everything seemed to be going well.

Then it all changed as he brought the final window frame into the house.

He stepped into the hallway, and as he did, he caught his right foot on the edge of the step and fell forward. The frame turned sideways with his weight against it and fell against the wall. It ripped a long tear through the wallpaper as it slid downward, coming to a stop just before hitting the floor. The glass inside remained intact.

"I'm lucky," he said to himself. But he wasn't.

He reached down and grabbed the frame with both hands. Now, he was ready to walk into the dining room. What he didn't see was the lace on his right shoe, which had come untied. In fact, that was the reason he had fallen seconds earlier when he had stepped on it and lost his balance.

This time, when he walked forward, he wasn't as fortunate.

Bobby couldn't believe what he was seeing.

He saw Mr. McGillicuddy's shoe lace twisting across the floor in front of his right shoe, and that's when disaster struck.

Mr. McGillicuddy tripped again, and this time, when he fell sideways he let loose of the frame with one hand and tried to place it on the floor to break the fall, but was unsuccessful.

Smash!

The pane inside broke immediately, and pieces of glass went flying into the dining room and the foyer, and even into the bedroom hallway. Flicker, Shining, and Dimmer just missed being hit.

Bobby ducked as a sliver flew over him.

"*Ouch,*" yelled his tiny little cousin, Whitening.

"*What happened?*" Bobby shouted.

"You ducked, and I got hit."

"Sorry, Whitening. Does it hurt?"

"Just a little, but I'm okay. You know me, Bobby. It hit right where I'm chipped. You can't make me any whiter than I am on that part of my body."

"Yeah! White on white," Bobby said. Then they laughed.

But it was not a laughing matter for Mr. McGillicuddy.

Bobby heard words coming from him that he had never heard before. He thought they might be naughty words.

He was embarrassed. He got up and checked his left wrist. It hurt a little and there were a couple of scratches on it, but he knew it could have been worse. The glass lay everywhere. Broken pieces had scattered clear into the bedroom hallway, and the still soggy carpet in the dining room was covered with little white specks.

"So, that's what happened," he said, as he looked down at his shoes while brushing off some more bits of glass that were clinging to his trousers. "My shoe is untied."

He looked at the frame and realized there was more bad news. When he had fallen, it had cracked the bottom.

"I'll have to call and order another one." Mr. McGillicuddy liked talking to himself when he was alone, and he continued, "I guess I better wait to install the other frames until I go get a new one."

He brushed glass from the rest of his trousers with a handkerchief he had taken from his back pocket. As he walked into the kitchen, more silvery flecks dropped to the floor.

He sat down and made the call to Lowe's.

"Poor Mr. McGillicuddy," Bobby chuckled.

"Now what?" asked Twinkle.

Bobby proceeded with the story. *"He said he was going to take a shower and forget about what happened."*

"Did he tell you that personally?"

"No, my comedian cousin, Bingo, but you know Mr. McGillicuddy. I've told you before. He loves to talk to himself."

"So what did he say?" Uncle Flicker's voiced boomed from the foyer.

"Well, he can't do anything else today in the dining room. When he called the store to order a new frame, they told him there were no more available. He has to wait two more days before he can get another one."

"Poor Mr. McGillicuddy," Bobby's mom said.

"So," Bobby continued, "After he walked through the kitchen and looked at the mess one more time, he went through the living room muttering to himself that he was going to take a shower. He said it would make him feel better."

"Anything else, Brother?"

"No, Dimmer, except for the fact that he's wishing now he hadn't tried to do any of this on his own."

"How do you know that?"

"Mr. McGillicuddy," Bobby raised his voice to make sure all heard, "apparently asked the man on the other end of the phone, if the store could send someone out immediately to fix the window. I don't know what the man said, but Mr. McGillicuddy was upset and yelled at him, 'What do you mean, a five week wait?'

"Then he moaned, and started asking the person he was talking to, if he could speak with the manager. That didn't do any good because he got mad and said, 'I'm bringing this van back, and I'm never shopping there again.'

"But only a couple of seconds later, he was apologizing to the person and promising that he didn't mean what he said. And then," Bobby laughed, "to finally top everything off, Mr. McGillicuddy says, 'If you can't fix the window, could you fix my front door?'"

"He doesn't understand the word 'no', does he?" chimed in Aunt Glaring, who had been smiling the entire time Bobby had told the story.

"No, and to make it even funnier, Mr. McGillicuddy said, 'In that case, I'll just do it myself. I don't really need any help.'"

Then the bulbs had something else to laugh about.

Mr. McGillicuddy had just stepped out of the shower and dried off when he thought he heard noises. "Is that someone talking?" he muttered to himself, as he opened the bathroom door that led into the master bedroom. He peered through the room and down the hall. Nothing there except the bulbs that had been kicked into the hallway by the firemen. He noticed two of the pictures were hanging crooked on the wall, victims of the wind that had rushed through the house during the tornado.

"Maybe I should leave those bulbs lying there until Jane returns home, so she can see what saved her."

He opened the armoire drawer and got some clean underwear and socks, and while he got dressed, he continued to talk to himself. "I need to hurry and return that van or I'm going to be charged $20 for keeping it too long."

It was dark outside and Mr. McGillicuddy sat alone at the kitchen table. After returning the van to Lowe's and stopping off at the hospital to see his wife, he had returned home.

It was 8 o'clock. He had eaten some soup and now stared at the empty bowl in front of him on the kitchen table. His attention drifted between the bowl and the newspaper in his right hand. He sipped on a diet coke and intermittently read news accounts about the tornado and the millions and millions of dollars of damage. It was still front-page news. When he looked at some of the photographs, he realized how fortunate they were that only the front part of their home had been struck.

Finally, he had read enough, and he put the newspaper aside. Lying in front of him on the table to his left, was a white sheet of paper. At the top was written: *Things to Do*. Beneath the headline were ten items. Number one read: "Pick up the materials" A big checkmark was beside it. Number two read: "Replace dining room window." A small checkmark was there with a question mark to its side. The rest of the list involved repair and cleanup projects at the house. None had yet been attempted.

He stood up and took the bowl to the sink and ran water over it. "Time to start making progress. I'll get the door put up tonight. Then I'll get some sleep and finish everything on this list, except the dining room, by tomorrow evening. I'm sure looking forward to Jane getting home. She'll be surprised at how much I've gotten done."

He walked into the foyer and tore off part of the plastic that covered the eight-foot tall oak door. Putting on a rich dark chocolate brown stain similar to the old door would come later. Right now, Mr. McGillicuddy's first chore was to remove the piece of plywood, which covered the front door entrance.

He managed to do it, but not without another crisis.

With only a small claw hammer in his hand, Mr. McGillicuddy started pulling the wood free from where it was nailed, but the hammer was not strong enough. Most people would have used a crowbar, but Mr. McGillicuddy didn't own one.

Fifteen minutes after he started, the plywood was ripped and torn around the edges, but, in most places, was not loose from where it had been nailed.

So, Mr. McGillicuddy decided to try and pull it away from the top of the door. He climbed up the steps of the ladder, but he slipped near the top and one of his legs fell in between two of the steps. It took him nearly two minutes to get his leg loose. After reaching the top, he spent a few more minutes tearing the plywood from the doorframe. Finally, after another 15 minutes, the covering was completely removed. He leaned it against the wall and tried to steady it, but it looked like it would fall at any moment.

And that's exactly what happened.

When he grabbed the ladder and started to take it to the garage, his foot caught on the hammer, which he had mistakenly laid on the floor. He slipped and fell, and so did the ladder, which hit the plywood and knocked it toward the floor. It looked like some giant magical carpet floating through the air as it fell on top of clumsy Mr. McGillicuddy.

Kerplunk!

"Ouch!" he squealed "My shoulder. I hurt my shoulder." He was lying on his back and the plywood was on top of him. Even though he was well over six feet tall, his body was completely covered.

He shoved the wood away angrily. He rolled to his right, but quickly turned the other way. "Oh boy, that hurts!"

He got up slowly and touched his right shoulder, which ached and felt like someone had jabbed him with a sharp object.

"How can I be so stupid?"

His shoulder ached, so he sat down dejectedly on the landing at the foot of the staircase near the front door. He rubbed his shoulder, but only for a second. It hurt to even touch it.

"Now look what I have done," he said, and walked back through the foyer and into the kitchen. He got a diet coke from the refrigerator. When he pulled the tab on the can with his right hand, pain shot to his shoulder. It ached and so did the ribs on his right side. He realized he had failed to put the heating gel on that morning.

He slumped into the chair at the built-in desk and turned on the small TV set to channel fifty five so he could see the nine o'clock news. The aftermath of the tornado took up the entire newscast. Every story had scenes of workers cleaning up debris and making repairs to houses and other buildings, as reporters spoke about the great progress being made throughout the city.

"I'm glad somebody is," he said to himself. "I'm certainly not." And with that, he turned off the television, dragged the ladder into the garage. Then he headed to the bedroom to get some sleep.

12

Mr. McGillicuddy Goofs Again

An exhausted Mr. McGillicuddy slept until 9:30 in the morning. When he rolled over to get out of bed, the aches from last night were still with him.

He wasted no time in putting some more heating gel on his ribs, just as he had done before going to sleep. "Might as well try it on my shoulder too." And he did.

"No reason to take a shower with all this smelly stuff all over me," he said. The salve was powerful. When he inhaled, the heat penetrated his nostrils and it went deep into his lungs.

Within minutes he felt better, and he headed for the kitchen. But just as he was reaching for the cereal box in the pantry, he realized what he had forgotten to do after the accident last night.

"Oh my gosh! I left the front door open."

Of course, it didn't make any difference now, after he had slept all night with the house unlocked. Nevertheless, he raced into the foyer.

There in front of him was the scene he had left when he went to bed. The shattered glass door stood wide open for anyone to enter, had they cared to, and the results of his mistakes and clumsiness were quite evident.

It was enough to make a man go eat breakfast. And that's exactly what he did.

"And then, I'm going to get that new door up and get some things done today," he said optimistically.

Bobby and the other bulbs had a good night's sleep too. They were awake when Mr. McGillicuddy came into the foyer. When he returned to the kitchen, they all wanted Bobby to tell them what he had said.

Bobby was laughing too hard to answer.

"Come on, Bobby, tell us," said Uncle Flicker.

When Bobby finally quit laughing, he told them.

Then all the bulbs laughed and Bobby said, *"I'll have to see it to believe it."*

"First things first," Mr. McGillicuddy murmured to himself, as he drug the piece of broken plywood from the house to the street side curb. He laid it on top of the broken window frame, a reminder of his accident in the dining room yesterday. Beneath those two items were a few small tree branches and some debris he had swept off the driveway.

He looked down the street, and on both sides there were much bigger piles of branches, and larger limbs. There were badly damaged pieces of furniture in front of three houses.

Just that scene alone made him again realize how lucky they had been. Especially Jane, he thought.

His shoulder was feeling better. His ribs ached only slightly.

"I'm ready to get that door put up." He hurried back inside.

There were three hinges, each about six inches long with three holes for screws, which needed to be attached to the wooden frame of the doorway.

Mr. McGillicuddy had an easy time with the first panel. Using a long screwdriver, he turned the first two screws into the wooden frame with no problem. The third one was tougher, but he put a lot of pressure on the screwdriver as he turned it and was able to get it solidly into the doorframe.

He then rechecked his measurements to make sure that where he was putting the second hinge panel was at the correct height from the floor. It had to match up perfectly so the other part of the hinge would connect.

Again, he had no trouble with the first screw, but then things got worse. With the head of the Phillips screwdriver in his mouth, he placed the tip of the second screw into the middle hole in the hinge plate. Then he held the plate with two fingers of his right hand and placed his thumb on the screw. With his left hand he took the screwdriver out of his mouth and realized he was holding it in the wrong hand.

He put the screwdriver back in his mouth, and with the thumb and forefinger of his left hand held the screw in the tiny hole.

"Now I'm ready," he mumbled, but he wasn't because the screw suddenly slipped from his grasp and fell to the floor.

"Dadblastit! Where did that screw fall? I can't find it. It's got to be here somewhere." He knelt down and ran his fingertips through the still damp and ruined Persian rug.

After two minutes of groping, griping, and grumbling, he finally found it.

This time he had more luck placing the handle of the screwdriver between his teeth, while using his left thumb and forefinger to hold the screw. He then easily took the screwdriver with his right hand, and was able to rotate the screw solidly into the wall.

"Ready for number three," said Mr. McGillicuddy.

He took the final screw out of the small plastic package, and in the fastest time yet, turned it deeply into the wood.

"Now, I've got things cooking," he said, obviously enjoying the conversation with himself and the fact he was making progress.

He placed the final hinge against the inside of the frame and very quickly was able to get the first two screws entered into the holes. He wasn't as lucky on the third one. It popped out of his hand, and went flying across the rug, rolling under an antique sewing machine that sat in a small alcove in the foyer.

Impatient to finally get something fixed, Mr. McGillicuddy decided not to try to find the screw. "The heck with it. Those hinges' are fine." But of course, he was wrong.

He walked over to where the door leaned against the pillar. With great care he stretched both arms across its three-foot wide front, and grasping it with both hands, he "duck-walked" it 15 feet to the doorway.

It was a heavy door, and even though Mr. McGillicuddy was 6'2", it took some grunting and groaning to lift it. He leaned the top part of the door to the right and tried to get the three spaces on the top door hinge to intermesh properly with the spaces on the just-installed hinge plate.

He was successful, but the weight of the door made his shoulder ache. He took a moment to stretch his right arm, as he balanced the door with his left hand.

"Two more to go and this big baby will be up and mounted." The brief rest was all he needed. He felt good, but that feeling lasted for only a moment.

He suddenly realized that when he had released his hold on the door to stretch his right arm, the door had tilted toward him. Now it began to move forward. He leaned into it and the weight of his body momentarily delayed the shifting of the door. It was then he heard a creak for the first time. What he didn't see, though, was the plate on the inside of the doorframe start to pull loose.

His attention was on trying to maneuver the two middle hinges together.

More than once he had them lined up. But each time he appeared to have them connected, they slipped free.

Finally, on about the fifth try, with sweat running down his forehead and his t-shirt beginning to show drops of perspiration, he lined the hinges correctly and they connected.

He let out a sigh of relief. "Just one to go. This one should be a piece of cake." He wiggled the bottom of the door ever so slightly and tried to line up the hinges, but they didn't connect.

He tried again unsuccessfully, and then he tried four more times. After each failed effort, he would wipe the sweat away from his eyes.

"Dadblastit!"

It was one of his favorite words when he was frustrated and couldn't get something to work. It was a word he often used.

"Dadblastit!"

Then he had an idea that he was sure would work. "I'll put the connecting bolts in the first two hinges and then the bottom one will have to connect."

He would need the ladder to reach the top hinge, so he hurried to the garage to get it, wondering why he had ever taken it back to the garage last night.

Bobby had heard Mr. McGillicuddy groaning and grunting, and occasionally heard the word "Dadblastit".

He didn't know what it meant, but he sure knew Mr. McGillicuddy wasn't happy.

Moments ago he had heard the strange word two more times, and then saw Mr. McGillicuddy suddenly race past the dining room and disappear through the door to the garage.

He had only been gone for a few seconds when Bobby heard a loud crash from inside the garage.

At the same moment, even though he couldn't see the front door, he heard another loud creeeeak!

Mr. McGillicuddy opened the door to the garage and quickly walked around the car to the far corner. Paint cans were sitting in front of the ladder. He pushed them aside with his foot, and, as he pulled on the ladder, it hit the side of a shelf. A nearly empty paint can came tumbling to the floor.

"Now what?" Mr. McGillicuddy grumbled. "What else can happen?"

He immediately found out.

Creeeak! The noise came from inside the house. "What's that?" he said, as he dragged the ladder to the back of the car.

Just as he was standing it upright so he could carry it in the house, he heard a much louder Creeeeeak! Then came the sound of something crashing to the floor.

"What the..." He dropped his hold on the ladder, and it fell against the car, scraping the trunk before falling to the concrete floor. Mr. McGillicuddy didn't even notice. His attention was focused on the noise.

He ran back inside and hurried through the hallway and past the dining room. As soon as he looked in the foyer, his mouth flew open, and he covered his face with both hands. He didn't want to look again, but of course, he had to do just that.

He slowly spread his fingers and peeked between them, but then quickly covered his eyes once more. He hoped the nightmare would disappear. But, when he took his hands down, it was still there in front of him. In frustration, he let out a loud shrieking sound and dropped down on his knees.

Lying on the floor was the brand new door. He looked to where it had stood, partially attached to the hinges, just one minute earlier.

Now the hinges were gone, ripped free from the paneling when the door had crashed to the floor. He saw one of them.

"How did this happen?" he shouted.

Then, he saw the other two hinges lying against the baseboard of the wall beneath the staircase. On one of the hinges, a screw dangled from a hole. All of the other screws were missing.

"I must not have screwed the plates into the wall tight enough." He glanced back at the opening where the door had teetered on the hinges just a couple of minutes earlier, and saw large holes and pieces of wood torn free from the inside of the frame. "The wood must have already been damaged due to the tornado." It was easier for him to believe that was the reason rather than admit to himself he was just a big goofus.

"I'll have to get that fixed by someone who knows how to do it." It was at that moment he turned his head and discovered more problems.

"No! No! No!"

He looked at the already splintered hand railing on the staircase and realized the thick post, which supported the railing at the bottom of the stairs, was also broken.

"Is there anything else that can go wrong?" he yelled to the empty room as he reached down and pulled the door up on its side and looked at the side nearest him. Everything appeared okay, so he lifted his right foot over it and, while holding the door with both of his hands so it wouldn't fall, put his other foot over it and held on tightly. Then he looked at the other side.

It was covered with many scratches, and there were huge dents near the top. When the hinges had pulled free from the panel, the door caromed off the pointed top of the stairwell post and was punctured.

Even so, he was certain it was salvageable. "I'm sure this can be fixed. I'll stain it, and no one will ever see the dents."

Less than 30 seconds later, he realized the sad truth when he pulled a large piece of plastic away from the lower portion of the door and saw a huge deep cut in the middle of the door.

At that point he lifted his face into the air, and in frustration let out a loud yell.

Later in the day, Mr. McGillicuddy carried more trash to the curb. Included in the debris was the imported Persian rug Mrs. McGillicuddy loved so much. There was no reason to keep it. It was badly ripped in two or three places, along with heavy water damage.

He brought the big sheet of plywood back into the house because he realized he would need it to cover the front door entrance. Sleeping with the door wide open was not a mistake he intended to make again tonight.

On his last trip to the street, as the clouds overhead rumbled with thunder, he took the dented door which he had purchased one day earlier and managed to destroy only a few hours later.

It wouldn't be used for firewood, although the thought had crossed his mind. He decided not to let Jane know he had bought it.

Earlier in the day, he had called Lowe's. They agreed to take three of the window frames back and refund him the money. Of course, he lost the money for the one he damaged and threw away.

Since the frames wouldn't fit in his car, he had to rent the van to return the frames.

When he got back from Lowe's, he picked up more sticks, limbs, leaves, and other trash that had blown into the front yard and stuffed all of it into large green trash bags. After moving the bags to the edge of the street where a huge pile of trash had accumulated, he paused and looked at the front yard, which was now free of the storm's debris. It was actually starting to look neat again.

But the house was a different story. He felt dejected as he stared at the huge plastic sheet covering the opening for the dining room window and the broken glass door at the entrance.

He noticed the gutter above the garage was packed full of leaves. That was a chore he might be able to do before it got dark within the next half hour.

"It would just make things nicer for Jane when she comes home tomorrow," he mumbled as he walked up the driveway and into the garage.

A call within the last hour had confirmed the hospital was releasing her. He would go see her for a few minutes later this evening and then return to pick her up around 8 o'clock tomorrow morning.

If he hurried he could be finished before sunset and maybe avoid the rain, which seemed more certain with each sound of thunder.

After bringing the ladder outside, he placed it on the left side of the front of the garage, put on his gloves, and with a roll of plastic trash bags in his hand, he climbed to the top of the ladder. In his back pocket was a small trowel.

Mr. McGillicuddy went right to work scooping out leaves with the tiny spade. As he pulled them out of the gutter, he flung the leaves to the driveway below. After four or five scoops, he suddenly remembered he had brought the trash bags with him.

He laid the trowel down, picked up the roll, and tore off a green bag. That part was easy. It was much harder to open the other end of the bag while wearing gloves and balancing on the steps of the ladder.

He tore at the end of the bag, but it wouldn't open. In frustration, he threw it to the ground and took another one out of the box. Once he found the perforated slit, he tore it loose and looked for the opening at the other end.

Finally, five minutes later, he had a bag open. He was using his hands and scooping the leaves into it. They were wet and packed together in clumps that easily fell to the bottom of the bag. Because they were so damp, it didn't take long for the bag to get heavy.

He dropped it down to the driveway and then scampered down the stairs to move the ladder to the middle of the gutter. He kicked the bag to the side of the garage.

Back to the top he climbed but he knew he needed to hurry if he was to finish before dark. After shoveling three more handfuls into the bag, he leaned to the right and tried to dig loose some mud that was in the bottom of the gutter. He hit at it with the tip end of the trowel but couldn't get it to come apart.

It was going to be necessary to lean farther to the right if he was going to be able to knock some more leaves down to the ground. When he was finished, Mr. McGillicuddy planned to pick them up.

"One more try and I think I can get that hunk of mud out of there, but I've got to get a better grip," he muttered. He took his gloves off and tossed them to the side of the garage. Then, moments later, he wished someone was there to hear him.

He stretched far to his right and held the trowel as tightly as possible, while batting at the caked mud wrapped around the leaves. As he took another hard chop, his right foot slipped on the step, and he started to fall but was able to grab for the gutter. When he did, he pulled the ladder sideways, it tilted to the right, and his left leg got caught between the fourth and fifth steps from the top of the ladder.

He grabbed the gutter with both hands, and, the trowel fell to the driveway and bounced into some nearby bushes.

The weight of his body began to pull the gutter loose from the edge of the roof. The ladder leaned farther to the right and looked like it would fall to the ground. He quickly managed to hook his right leg tightly against the steps.

Now hanging by both hands and pushing backward with his feet, he somehow kept the ladder from falling. But he couldn't last long. His fingers were hurting. The gutter was cutting into them.

He dangled there, trying desperately to reach up with his left hand and get some traction on the roof so he could pull himself up. Then he heard her voice.

"What in the world are you doing, John McGillicuddy?"

Tromping across the street was his neighbor, Phyllisjean. "Are you trying to kill yourself," she shouted, and began to walk faster toward him.

"Can you pull the ladder back under me?" he groaned.

"I'm hurrying." She reached the ladder and tried to straighten it. "You've got to help, John. I can't do this unless you try to drag it with your leg."

Suddenly there was a loud screeching sound.

"Help me," he shrieked, as the gutter ripped off of the edge of the roof. At that very instant, by nothing but a miracle, as she would call it later, Phyllisjean pulled the ladder underneath him just in time.

He was able to grab the edge of the roof with his left hand, just as his hat came loose and floated down toward the driveway. Seconds later he managed to get both feet on the steps, just as the gutter crashed to the driveway.

"Oh my goodness!" She looked more frightened than Mr. McGillicuddy.

He steadied himself for a moment at the top and then slowly stepped down to the driveway. He hugged and thanked her for saving him, and then, in the same breath, he looked her in the eyes and said, "Don't tell Jane this happened. Let me handle it. I'm so embarrassed."

Phyllisjean nodded her head, accepted his thanks, and walked back across the street. "He's always playing jokes on me," she whispered to herself as she walked up her driveway. "Does he really think I won't tell Jane?"

13

Mrs. McGillicuddy Comes Home

When the car rounded the corner, Mrs. McGillicuddy got her first look at the house. As the
auto turned into the driveway, she moaned, "Oh, John!
How awful! Just look at that plastic hanging over the
window, and the front door torn away, and the gutter
lying in the driveway."

Bobby heard the garage door open. He knew it was
mid-morning because he had been able to hear most of
Mr. McGillicuddy's telephone conversation a few hours
earlier at six o'clock. Mr. McGillicuddy had reminded
his brother-in-law during the very quick visit on the
phone that he had to be at the hospital at seven o'clock
so he could bring Mrs. McGillicuddy home.

Bobby had also heard Mr. McGillicuddy say he needed to pick up some prescription medicine after he left the hospital.

Now, Bobby saw the door from the garage open. He had a perfect view from the bedroom hallway at the other end of the house.

"*There she is,*" he whispered to his mom, whose vision to the door was blocked.

"*I see her too,*" Uncle Flicker chipped in.

"*Me too, Bobby,*" said Aunt Shining.

Mrs. McGillicuddy walked into the dining room leaning heavily on the cane she would use during her recovery from her bruised hip. There was a huge bandage on her right leg. It ran from the top of her foot almost to her knee.

She stood there only a few seconds, and then she began to cry when she noticed the painting that she loved so much was missing.

Stepping on the soggy ruined carpet gave her even more reason to cry, and when she saw her once beautiful cherry wood dining room table, which had been in the family for over 100 years, the tears poured down her cheeks.

"Oh, John. The whole dining room set is destroyed. Look at it."

"We'll get it fixed or replaced, Jane," he said.

"I hope so." She pulled a handkerchief out of her purse and started wiping her face. "The insurance company better pay for this, especially since we've hardly ever had any claims."

"That won't make any difference, dear. We'll get it paid for."

"I just want it to look like it always did." Then she started to sniffle again.

Mr. McGillicuddy wrapped his arms around his wife and pulled her close. He could see the tears streaming down her cheeks.

"Listen closely to me, Jane," he said. "We will eventually get the house repaired."

"I know," Mrs. McGillicuddy said, and she started to pull loose from her husband. "Just let me look at everything else."

Mr. McGillicuddy did not remove his arms but held her tight. He took his right hand and placed it under her chin and tilted her face up toward his. "Listen to me, and then we will finish looking at the house. Everything in here is important to us. It brings back many memories. When we get the new furniture, and the house is repaired, these things will become a part of our memories in the future. The new paint, and new windows, and new rugs, and new wallpaper will all be marvelous. But, the most important thing is, you are in my arms, you are okay, and you are alive. Don't ever forget that. None of the rest is important if you aren't here.

He released her and turned to walk down the hallway. "Come on, let's get you to the bedroom so you can lie down and rest."

But she just stood there for a few more seconds looking at the dining room. Finally, she turned and walked into the foyer. Now the tears really began to roll down her cheeks.

"The rug is ruined in here, too. Where's my Persian rug?"

"It's at the curb, dear, torn and ripped into pieces."

"My heavens, how did that get broken?" She was staring at the staircase railing for the first time.

"Well, the storm, of course," said Mr. McGillicuddy. He didn't offer to tell the whole story.

Her eyes shifted to the plywood covering the door. "John," she said, "I thought you told me we had a new door and you were going to put it up."

"Huh!" he paused, "Well, not everything has gone as smoothly as I wanted."

"What does that mean, dear?"

"What it means is, I will tell you later after you've rested."

"Okay, but what did you get done?" she asked, as she turned the corner in the foyer and began limping toward the bedroom hallway. "Oh, my gosh. I almost stepped on these bulbs. John, why are they still here? I thought you said you threw out a lot of our bulbs because they were broken."

"I did, I did," he stammered.

"Well, you mean you didn't have time in two days to unplug these bulbs and put them someplace?"

"Jane, I told you at the hospital what happened. These bulbs may have saved your life. I just wanted you to see them. I want them to be on our Christmas tree for as long as we are together." Then he went and put his arms around her, almost stepping on the two bulbs closest to the outlet in the process.

"Come on, dear, let's get you to bed and get you some rest."

She stepped over the bulbs and started to walk down the hallway, but she stopped. "John, please put these bulbs up. I'm confused. I've heard your story. Heard it three times, as a matter of fact, at the hospital. So again, try to explain to me how these bulbs ended up plugged into a wall socket. And, if you can do that, explain how they were lit and actually shining after a tornado. Just think about it, John. How could they end up in a packed knot on my leg. I mean, according to you, all of the medical people said it may have kept me from bleeding to death. It is scary, very scary, and yet it's almost like a miracle."

"I know, Jane. I've thought about it myself. Something very strange happened, although you know how many weird things go on during tornadoes. Like all those stories we've heard over the years of someone's house not having damage, and the house next door will be demolished. Or, how about the Gonzalez' down the street? I heard they had one half of their living room lifted out of the house. The sofa was sucked into the sky, but the table next to it was untouched and the lamp on it was still shining."

Mrs. McGillicuddy was only half listening as she slowly walked down the hallway, putting a lot of weight on her cane with each step. She stopped at the bedroom door and looked back over her shoulder at the strand of bulbs on the floor. "Maybe those bulbs are related to that lamp," she said, and then, for the first time since she had arrived at her house, she smiled and laughed quietly.

14

The long Cleanup

During her first day home, Mrs. McGillicuddy insisted Mr. McGillicuddy remove the broken railing and the staircase post and take them outside.

Because none of the major repair projects were started, she became very impatient with Mr. McGillicuddy, although there was little he could do.

She had asked him to go buy a new front door and install it himself, because due to the tornado, every repairman and carpenter in town were six weeks behind in their appointments.

Mr. McGillicuddy had explained that Lowe's and Home Depot did not have the size of door they needed, plus there was a shortage of supplies and materials everywhere. He wasn't certain all of that was true, but he didn't mind believing it because he didn't want to try putting up a new door again, and he had no intention of letting Mrs. McGillicuddy know he had already damaged one door beyond repair.

A week had passed since she had left the hospital, and Mrs. McGillicuddy was finally getting around to cleaning up the rest of the mess in the foyer. She had picked up the last of the special ornaments that were scattered throughout the closet and put them in the box. Two strands were still on the floor in the foyer, and she picked them up and placed them in the box with the other bulbs. The other strand was still partially plugged into the wall socket. She now called them her "miracle" bulbs, and she put them on top of all the other strands at the top of the box.

This had pleased Mr. McGillicuddy very much. "I want to know where those bulbs are when it's time to decorate the Christmas tree," he had said.

It was many weeks later, and the storage box remained in the living room as the McGillicuddys waited for their house to be repaired.

Bobby had turned out to be the luckiest of all the bulbs. After Mrs. McGillicuddy had wound the strand in a tight coil, Bobby, his folks, and Aunt Glaring, had ended up at the very top. Bobby, nearest the edge, could see everything in the room and all the way to the front door.

He wondered, based on all the other conversations he had heard, if the house was ever going to be repaired. Actually, he didn't mind because the longer it took, the longer they remained outside of the closet.

After nearly a month and a half had passed, there was still no remodeled dining room, no new window, no new front door, no new gutter, and no freshly painted house. It was May 19th and the McGillicuddys celebrated their 35th wedding anniversary by having dinner in the kitchen. They reminisced of wonderful moments in their lives, and, smiling, gave each other a kiss. And then Mrs. McGillicuddy asked, "Are we going to be the last house on the street to return to normal?"

It was a question she asked every day.

Just after the middle of June, Mrs. McGillicuddy's question was finally answered.

Monday, June 18th was Mr. McGillicuddy's birthday, and the house still waited to be repaired. But a day later, the good news finally came. Mrs. McGillicuddy answered the telephone around noon. When she hung up, she told her husband, "It's a day late, but I have a birthday present for you. The workmen are coming tomorrow, and they want to get everything done by Saturday night."

She was so excited she wanted to share the good news with her friend and neighbor, Phyllisjean. As she hurried outside and began to cross the street, she looked down the block and saw five other houses, which had been severely damaged during the tornado. They all appeared to be completely repaired. In fact, with fresh paint and newly laid bricks, they looked like recently built homes.

"How did this happen?" she said to herself as she walked up her neighbor's driveway. "Every house in the neighborhood is repaired, and they are just starting on ours."

She rang Phyllisjean's doorbell. When her friend came to the door, Mrs. McGillicuddy told her the good news. They visited for about five minutes, and then, as she was starting to leave, her neighbor whispered something to her. "Are you serious?" Mrs. McGillicuddy asked before walking away.

When she came through the garage and walked into the house, she hollered, "John, would you come here and talk to me?" A moment later he came to the hall-way. "Follow me, honey," she said.

The overhead garage door was open, and they walked outside. She turned and looked up at the roof. Mr. McGillicuddy stood beside her, and his eyes moved upward too. Then she gently stuck her elbow into his ribs and looked him squarely in the eyes. "You didn't tell me why the gutter was missing, John."

"What do you mean, dear?"

"Don't play innocent with me. Did you have some problems while attempting to repair the gutter?"

"Uhhh ... Well, uhhh ... "

"Yes, I'm waiting," she said, but a smile broke out on her face.

"Okay," Mr. McGillicuddy said, and he tucked his head downward.

"Go ahead, John. Look me in the eyes. It won't be hard to say."

Then John McGillicuddy started to laugh. "Yes, dear. You are definitely married to a klutz. I did have a few problems with the gutter, and for that matter the front door, and some windows, too."

Then he took his hand and placed it around Mrs. McGillicuddy's waist. They walked out to the curb, and then back along the driveway and into the garage. Mr. McGillicuddy confessed a few of the many things he had done wrong during the cleanup after the tornado.

By the time they returned inside the house, they were laughing. Mrs. McGillicuddy pinched Mr. McGilllicuddy on the ear and said with a smile, "See, that wasn't so difficult to tell the truth, was it?"

15

The Workmen Finally Arrive

"**W**hat's happening, Bobby?" "What do you want to know, Uncle Flicker?"

"Not just me, we all want to know. We can hear the noise. Are there a bunch of people here?"

"Oh, yes!" Bobby twisted himself upright so he could see even better. "I have a great view."

It was 7:30 Wednesday morning when the first workmen arrived. It was evident they wanted to finish everything by the weekend as they had predicted. Two hours later, there were work crews everywhere in the dining room, the living room, the foyer, and on the staircase. The house was abuzz with activity.

From where the box was sitting, Bobby could see everything in the foyer, the dining room, and part of the stairwell.

"*They just finished the dining room window. It took them less than two hours, and that's after they had removed all of the furniture. Poor Mrs. McGillicuddy, she's been sobbing every time she walks through the hallway.*"

"*She loved that table,*" Bobby's mom chipped in.

"*What happened?*" It was Uncle Glimmer, who was way below Bobby and couldn't see anything.

"Remember," Bobby said, "*the table was ruined. There was too much water damage, and there were big dents on the top where glass and wood had slammed into it. They've already loaded it on a truck to be taken to the junkyard. The china cabinet and server both look like they will have to be worked on, but apparently can be saved. They are sitting behind us here in the living room. If they bring anything else in here, they will have to move our box.*"

Bobby hoped that didn't happen. Even though no one was happy about the damage to the house, it was still exciting to be able to see the workmen busily at work.

For nearly two hours he explained to the other bulbs what the workmen were doing. He also answered some questions until suddenly he whispered, *"Hush!"* He heard Mr. McGillicuddy in the hallway and saw him walking toward the box. Then Bobby watched him look down at the bulbs. He acted as if he wanted to say something.

Mr. McGillicuddy thought he heard something as he walked through the living room. "This is awful."

"Talking to yourself again, John?" Mrs. McGillicuddy chuckled as she walked up behind him.

He acted as if he hadn't heard her.

"Afraid to talk with me standing here?" she kidded him.

"All right, I was talking to myself," he admitted. "I was just looking at all this furniture crammed in here and wondering if I should take these boxes upstairs."

"You probably should," she answered. "Although we could put them back in the closet once it's refinished and painted."

"What was that noise?"

"What noise?" she asked.

"I just heard something from inside this box," he answered, and bent over to peer inside.

"John, are you crazy? What are you doing?"

He didn't answer.

"Will you tell me why you are tearing everything up in that box?"

"I'm not hurting anything. Just feeling around. I thought there might be a mouse or something down in there."

"A what?" she shrieked. "A mouse! Are you absolutely out of your mind?" She began to laugh, and each time she quit, she would start laughing again.

Mr. McGillicuddy just stood there looking at her like she was crazy. "What's so funny?" he demanded.

"You," she said, and then she was joined in laughter by a couple of the workmen who had witnessed Mr. McGillicuddy's silly antics.

Mr. McGillicuddy began to blush, and the redder he got, the more the three of them laughed.

"I just thought I heard something in the box." When the laughter continued, he stomped away and headed into the kitchen.

Now, Mrs. McGillicuddy looked inside the box. She saw where her husband had moved some ornaments, but the light strands were still neatly stacked, except for the one on top.

"Oh my!" she said as she looked closer. "My "miracle" bulbs must have gotten damaged during the storm.

"John, come back in here and look at this."

What Mr. McGillicuddy saw, when he returned to the living room, was his wife holding up the strand. She pointed to two bulbs. "See these bulbs. They were either stepped on or broken during the storm. You'll need to throw them out."

Mr. McGillicuddy nodded. "Okay, dear, but not now. The workers are going to lunch. Can you fix me something?"

"Why?" she remarked. "They did the work this morning, not you." She laughed, and reminded him, "Get those two bulbs replaced because this strand is going to be on Remington's tree."

"I will, I will, but just not now."

"Well, see that you get it done."

"I'll replace them after Thanksgiving when we decorate Remington's tree."

Bobby didn't know whether to thank Mrs. McGillicuddy, or be angry with her. He was so worried about his dad and Whitening, but at the same time very happy that the bulbs were going to be put on Remington's tree at Christmas.

He didn't want to frighten his mom and the rest of the family but he knew they would have to be told the whole story.

"This isn't easy to say but I have bad news." After he told her there was nothing but silence for a few seconds, and then his mom and some of the other bulbs began to cry.

Uncle Flicker shouted, *"You've got to do something, Bobby. You have five months to figure out a plan to save them."*

"Can you do it, Son?"

"I'll think of something, Mom. I have to. After all, I am Bobby Bright."

PART
THREE

16

Thanksgiving is Here

It was 75 days since the workers had repaired, painted, and wallpapered the damaged house. The ornaments and Christmas tree light bulbs had been placed in a new box inside the remodeled foyer closet. Bobby and the Bright family strand were at the top of the box, and Bobby could actually peer over the edge. During the day there was enough light shining under the closet door that he could see clothes hanging from the rack above and three suitcases and several boxes on the floor.

Even though it was a better view and the conditions were improved over previous years, the days still slowly passed by. Just as he had done so many times in the past 10 years, Bobby often wished for the time to speed up so the holiday season would arrive quicker. He was especially anxious this year because he so wanted to be back on Remington's tree again.

Then of course, there were times when he wished just the opposite. He would hope the time would pass slowly. Bobby needed more time to figure out a plan to save his dad and cousin Whitening once Mr. McGillicuddy took the bulbs out of the box.

But, as it happened every year, time did not stand still, it did not slow down, and it did not speed up. The big day arrived on time.

The McGillicuddys always decorated their tree the day after Thanksgiving. It was tradition.

However, Mrs. McGillicuddy didn't always cook on Thanksgiving. Occasionally, they would go to Mrs. McGillicuddy's brother's house for turkey dinner.

But this year, there was no question Thanksgiving dinner would be at the McGillicuddys. She wanted to show off her new cherry wood dining table and the eight beautiful chairs that circled it.

Earlier this Thanksgiving morning, Mr. McGillicuddy had been kept busy with lots of chores, including two trips to the grocery store to pick up things she had forgotten to buy earlier.

But finally, dinner was ready to be served. Each chair at the table was filled. Mrs. McGillicuddy's brother, Stan; his wife, Nancy; and their three children, along with neighbor Phyllisjean, joined the McGillicuddys. After a wonderful prayer from Mr. McGillicuddy, there was a momentary quiet as all eyes focused on the feast Mrs. McGillicuddy had prepared. She had worked since very early in the morning and there was turkey, mashed potatoes, green beans, corn, dressing, devilled eggs and four different pies to choose from.

"Dig in and enjoy yourself," she said, and they did. By the end of the dinner, which was filled with lots of laughter and loud talking, there was little left of what had been in front of them an hour ago. Mr. McGillicuddy was crowned the pie-eating champion, having managed to eat a slice of all four selections.

By late afternoon, everyone had told everyone else "Happy Thanksgiving" a number of times, and finally, the house became quiet after the guests had left.

"John, you were wonderful today," Mrs. McGillicuddy said.

"Thank you, my dear," he answered, "And now it's time to think about Christmas."

17

Out of the Box

It happened only two times a year—the day spring-cleaning started and the day after Thanksgiving.

The box with the special ornaments and lights was about to be picked up by Mr. McGillicuddy.

"*What a feeling!*" Bobby whispered to his mom and dad and brother and sisters.

At that moment, the box lifted into the air, and every member of the Bright family heard a grunt from Mr. McGillicuddy.

He moved slowly through the foyer, stepped down into the living room, and almost tripped. However, he managed to keep his balance and entered the room the McGillicuddy's called the sports arena. Inside were two large television sets, lots of chairs and sofas, and game tables. Some of the tables and chairs were shifted and moved to other corners of the room so there would be space for the eight-foot tall tree.

In past years, when they had been buried at the bottom of the box, the Bright family bulbs were shaken up and jostled around when the box was lowered to the floor. However, this year was different.

The bulbs barely moved when Mr. McGillicuddy sat the box on the floor near the tall Noble Fir. As he always did each year, on the day after Thanksgiving, he had purchased the tree earlier in the day. Last year had been the first year he had bought a second tree, a tiny Scotch Pine, which was put in the guest room for Remington. This year, Mr. McGillicuddy had again bought a small Scotch Pine for upstairs.

Even though Bobby had heard Mr. McGillicuddy say the strand was going to go upstairs to Remington's tree, Bobby wouldn't believe it until it happened.

The bulbs still had to be "tested" by Mr. McGillicuddy to make sure they would all light properly. That was always an adventure, especially when Mr. McGillicuddy would drink Mrs. McGillicuddy's eggnog.

He loved it, but it did make him sleepy and drowsy because her apple cinnamon recipe included freshly cut apples soaked in a special sauce with cinnamon. What made it special were the secret ingredients she added to make it spicier than any other eggnog. Everyone who drank it, loved it, whether it was served hot or cold.

"It is delicious," she would tell family and friends, "but it will make you sleepy because of all the sugar."

Bobby knew it not only made Mr. McGillicuddy drowsy, but it also made him goofy and clumsy, turning almost everything he did into an adventure.

Bobby peered over the top of the box and saw the tree in the corner. "*Wow,*" he said quietly, "*It's another big one.*" He remembered all those years when his strand had been the last out of the box, the first on the tree, and hidden at the very back from everyone's view.

All of that had changed last year. Now it was time to see if the wonderful Christmas from a year ago would be repeated.

Mr. McGillicuddy opened the box and looked at the top strand. He laughed and then yelled to his wife, who was in the kitchen taking dishes out of the dishwasher. "The 'miracle' bulbs are here, dear. Do you want me to test them like all the others, or do you think they automatically shine whether plugged in or not?"

"Oh, now you are making fun of me," she hollered back as she walked into the room, "But I see you've decided to test them anyway."

He grabbed the plug and shoved it into the wall socket near the tree. "I just want to make sure," he said.

The heat rushed into their bodies, just like it did every year when they were plugged in for the first time.

"Oh, that feels good."

"I'd forgotten how good it feels to be warm."

"We're on! We're on!"

"Quiet!" Bobby ordered, "I want to hear."

"Perfect. Just look at them, Jane," he said, and took a sip of eggnog from the mug in his hand.

"John McGillicuddy," she raised her voice, and stared at him with her hands on her hips.

He looked over the top of his mug and gulped. "What did I do?"

"It's not what you did, it's what you didn't do," she snapped back at him.

"Oh," he said sheepishly, and tucked his head downward, like a boy caught taking a cookie from the cookie jar.

Mrs. McGillicuddy was looking right at the broken bulb near the end of the strand.

"Didn't I tell you to replace those two broken bulbs? The top is gone from that one," she said and pointed toward the end of the strand, "and the one in the middle that's chipped and white looks silly laying next to all those colored bulbs."

"I know," Mr. McGillicuddy said, "it's just that they are some of the bulbs that helped save you."

"Oh, John, please! I know it was probably me who nicknamed them 'miracle' bulbs last spring, but you act like they are real people. Just be nice and replace the bad ones with two new colored bulbs and take the strand upstairs to Remington's tree."

He started to argue, but thought better of it. "Yes, dear."

"*What is it?*" his mom asked quietly.

"*Mrs. McGillicuddy told Mr. McGillicuddy to throw away the broken bulbs.*"

"*No!*" She screamed.

"*You've got to do something,*" said Dimmer.

"*It's always the same, I'm the one who has to do something.*"

"*Then do it,*" said his mom.

Mr. McGillicuddy stood looking down at the bulbs on the floor. He took a long swallow and emptied the last of the eggnog from his just refilled cup.

"What was that noise? Are you little bulbs talking to me like Remington claimed you did last Christmas?" He thought that was funny, and he laughed loudly. His attention remained on the very dark blue bulb near the end of the cord.

That one particular bulb mystified him, which he was certain was the same one he had seen on Remington's tree last year. If that was true, he thought, this was the same strand of bulbs his grandson had been convinced was doing mysterious things.

"Are you really 'miracle' bulbs?" He dropped down to one knee and started to reach for the blue bulb, when something happened that he would never forget for the rest of his life.

In the future, Bobby would remember this moment as the very instant when the idea to save his dad and Whitening finally began to take shape.

Mr. McGillicuddy was the bulbs' best friend. If Bobby could make him believe that these bulbs were so unique and special, then Bobby believed Mr. McGillicuddy would do nothing to hurt them.

He looked right at Mr. McGillicuddy and winked. It was better than either of the two winks he had given Remington last year. It was a "wink" that, at least for the moment, saved his dad and his sweet little cousin.

Mr. McGillicuddy jumped to his feet, and when he did, he dropped the empty mug on the floor.

"That blue bulb winked at me. Those other bulbs are all shaking. What's happening? If I tell Jane she'll think I'm crazy. I'm getting you guys upstairs." He reached down to pick them up, but jerked his hand back before touching the bulbs.

Instead, he walked over to where the mug lay on the carpet, bent over, and picked it up. He wanted to think this over, but he realized he didn't have time.

Mrs. McGillicuddy had gone to the garage to find one other small box of Christmas tree ornaments.

There was a decision to be made. After walking to the wall socket and jerking the plug loose, he hurried out of the room. He stepped into the sunken living room before racing through the foyer and up the stairs. From below he heard the door from the garage open. His wife shouted, "John, didn't you hear me calling you? Come help me!"

"Dad, calm down," Bobby interrupted. "*I think it's going to be okay. Keep your filaments crossed. I think you and Whitening are going to be with us for a long time.*"

"*Oh, Bobby! Is it really possible?*" his cousin shouted with joy from under Mr. McGillicuddy's left arm.

"*Not too loud,*" Bobby whispered, "*We don't want to scare Mr. McGillicuddy again.*"

18

Saved for the Moment

Mr. McGillicuddy hurried into the upstairs guest room. On the table just inside the door to his right, sat the tiny Scotch pine he had bought this morning.

With bulbs in hand, he stood in front of the table and looked at the little pine tree sitting upon it. When he spoke it was like he was talking to the tree. "You're better looking than Remington's tree last year," he said, "And your branches are thicker. The bulbs and ornaments will look prettier because the branches are so wide. Yep," he added, "I did a good job picking this one out."

"Talking to yourself again, John," Mrs. McGillicuddy said, as she entered the room. "You know, if people heard you like I do, they would think you are nuts."

"Just looking at this tree, dear. It is a pretty little thing."

"John, why didn't you come and help me? I yelled three times from the garage. Do you hear anything I say anymore?"

He didn't answer. He was too busy reaching behind the table and plugging in the extension cord.

"Apparently you don't."

"Don't what, dear?" He stared at her with a blank look on his face.

"I can't lift the box with the crystal ornaments. It's too heavy. Can you please get it and bring it inside?"

"I'll do it. Just give me a minute," he said, as he turned and shielded her view of the bulbs, which were in a clump on the floor. He looked back over his shoulder and smiled, "Okay?"

"Well hurry up. I want to start decorating the living room. By the way, did you take care of this strand like I told you?"

"I've got everything under control." As he said it, he looked to the floor, his body blocking her view, and with the toe of his right shoe, scooted the bulb with the broken top underneath some of the other ones. He turned and smiled, but she was already gone.

When he heard her reach the bottom of the stairs, he said to himself, "What a day! I see these bulbs shaking and looking like they are crawling along the floor like some kind of a snake. And then, I see that bulb wink at me. At least I thought it winked at me. And now, I think I'm hearing weird voices and sounds. Maybe I *am* going nuts."

He stood there without moving and stared at the bulbs. It was nearly a minute before he snapped out of the trance. Finally, he picked up the strand and neatly placed the bulbs throughout the branches.

It was evening. The bulbs could hear the music drifting from the big room downstairs.

It was tradition at the McGillicuddy's that every night, from the day after Thanksgiving until the day after Christmas, holiday music could be heard in the house for four hours beginning at six o'clock. The McGillicuddys had a large collection of songs and instrumentals from many different artists and seldom was a song repeated during the evening. However, there was one song that always played three or four times.

"Here comes the McGillicuddy's favorite again," Bobby said when he heard the introductory stanza of "Silent Night."

He remembered the McGillicuddys called it their "lucky" Christmas carol.

Bobby knew he needed some luck if he was going to save his dad and Whitening.

He tried to enjoy the music, but his mind wandered as the evening went along. The rest of the bulbs chatted in "Bulbese" and spoke about the McGillicuddy's Christmas party, called the "Big One," and hoped it would happen again. Over 50 people had seen the bulbs on the tiny tree last year when they had come to the party, and the bulbs had enjoyed shining for all the guests.

Finally, at ten o'clock the music stopped. The house became quiet, and most of the bulbs quickly fell asleep. It was then, in the stillness of the upstairs room, that an idea Bobby had earlier in the day began to take shape. As he considered the possibilities, his mom leaned to her left and touched him.

"Good night, Bobby!"

"Good night, Mom. I just hope tomorrow is a good day."

She didn't like the sound of that remark, but thought it was probably Bobby just worrying as usual.

19

Save Him, Bobby, Please!

"There's nothing better than warmed over Thanksgiving turkey, lots of gravy, and scrambled eggs. It's a wonderful tradition, Jane."

"Yes, dear, it certainly is. In fact, it lasts through the Thanksgiving weekend. Yesterday, you needed all this food so you would have enough energy to buy the trees, put them up, test the bulbs, and then help me decorate."

"Well, it worked," he said with a big smile.

"Good. Then it will work today. There is still plenty to do. You need to get out front and put the deer in the yard this morning. Plus, don't forget you are helping the man install the roof lights."

"Oh, yeah," he paused in the middle of a huge bite of turkey, part of it hanging from his lower lip, "I forgot. Couldn't the guy put them on the roof without me?"

"Yes, he could," Mrs. McGillicuddy answered without turning around to look at him. She continued to place the dirty dishes into the dishwasher.

"Then, why doesn't he?" Mr. McGillicuddy asked.

Mrs. McGillicuddy had turned to pick up the skillet from the stove when she saw him. "Do you see yourself?" She was looking at the hanging piece of turkey covered with gravy.

"What?"

"Your chin. Are you going to eat the gravy or do you plan to shave with it?"

He saw where she was pointing.

"Oh!" he said, as he took a napkin and removed the thick white mess lathered across his chin.

"As to your other question, John, you are going to help him so he doesn't charge us for four hours work when it can be done in an hour and a half. I love the lights trimmed around the house, but there's no reason to spend more money than necessary."

She started to walk out of the kitchen and then stopped for a moment. "Would you please put the rest of the dishes in the dishwasher before you leave? I'm going upstairs to put those extra ornaments on Remington's tree before Angie and Stacey call."

"Does that mean you are going shopping with them?"

"Of course. Those nutty people who want to fight all those crowds the day after Thanksgiving had their marathon yesterday. Now we normal people will shop today. Besides, it's our Saturday after Thanksgiving tradition."

"Except you three are such tightwads, and you never buy anything."

"That's why they call it shopping," she yelled from the foyer, and then laughed as she headed up the stairs.

Mr. McGillicuddy chuckled, wiped his chin one more time, and then stood up to take the dishes to the counter. He almost dropped them when he remembered.

"Oh my gosh!" He quickly placed them in the dishwasher and started to run out of the kitchen. The shout from above stopped him in his tracks.

"John McGillicuddy!"

He knew why she was angry. It was the reason he was already running up the stairs.

"*Wake up right now. Wake up, everybody!*" he called out to the other bulbs.

He didn't have a chance to say anymore. He saw her round the corner at the top of the staircase. She held a box in her hands with gold tinsel and beads hanging from one corner.

She placed the box on the edge of the bed directly across from the table.

Bobby saw her look at the tree. He saw the expression on her face and knew exactly where she was staring. Her eyes were darting back and forth between his dad and Whitening. Then, she yelled.

"*John McGillicuddy!*" The second time was even louder than the first.

She heard him scrambling up the stairs. When he rounded the corner, he had the look of a blameless little boy on his face.

"Don't give me that innocent look."

"What do you want? Are you okay? I thought something was wrong with you."

"You know what's wrong with me. Don't act like you don't know what's going on." Before he could answer, she placed her finger against the broken bulb near the front of the tree.

"Right there," she said. "Why is this bulb and the other one still on the tree? You told me you had changed them."

"I did not. I said everything was taken care of."

"Well, everything isn't taken care of because they are still here."

"Why are you so concerned? What difference does it make?"

"Do you think Remington wants broken bulbs on his tree? Plus, that one bulb couldn't possibly light. It's broken."

"I just thought they were special bulbs…." but he never had a chance to finish the sentence.

"Will you please quit acting like these bulbs can talk and are human. I'm going to take them off myself."

She reached for the broken one in front and started to unscrew it. "And you get the other one out of here right now."

Mr. McGillicuddy could barely squeeze between her and the foot of the bed. "Have you been putting on weight, Jane?" he asked as he stepped to the other side of the tree.

She frowned at him and handed him the bulb. "Real funny, John. Your attempt at humor won't save you this time. Finish unscrewing that bulb." She waited until he had done just that. "Now hand it to me. Where are the new ones?"

"In the top drawer, where I put them," he said, and pointed to the small dresser against the wall.

She brushed past him, grabbed the handle, and pulled the drawer open just as the phone rang from the nearby upstairs office.

Quickly, she reached in the drawer, grabbed the two colored bulbs inside, and tossed them and the broken bulbs onto the bedspread. The phone rang a second time as she shoved past Mr. McGillicuddy and headed into the hallway.

"Wow! When it's time to shop, everything takes a back seat, doesn't it? I guess these old bulbs aren't quite as bad now."

She ignored him and rushed into the office, picking up the phone just before the third ring.

Without taking time to say hello, she said, "Stacey, I hope you girls are ready for some shopping. Tell Angie to honk when she pulls into the driveway. I'll be right out."

When she hung up the phone and walked back to the bedroom doorway, she saw him staring at the tree.

"Now what?" she asked. "Think you hear more voices?" she laughed, and headed down the stairs.

"Actually, I think I did," he said quietly.

As she stepped into the foyer there was the sound of the doorbell chiming. She called up the stairs, "It's the light man, John. Come on down and tell him what we want done. Don't forget you are helping him."

"Let me tell you what's happening. Do you see the bulbs on the bedspread?"

The four bulbs were lying on the folded cover near the foot of the four-poster bed. Bobby saw the frightened looks on the faces of his dad and Whitening as they looked down from the bed.

"Will someone tell me what's going on?" bellowed Uncle Flicker.

"Just trust me," Bobby answered, "I've had an idea for a while, and now I think I may have time to pull it off. Here's my game plan."

"What are you, some kind of a coach?" Dimmer asked.

"Don't be cracking jokes right now, little brother."

"Oh, come on Bobby, you gotta be cool. The pressure is on. Don't get too uptight. You can do it. You're the man, Bobby!"

"Yeah! You're the man, Bobby," chanted the bulbs throughout the tree.

Mrs. McGillicuddy had taken time to show the man installing the lights how she wanted them placed around the house and on the tall maple tree in the front yard.

She was about to step back inside the house when she heard the honk of a horn and saw her sisters inside the car. It nearly hit Mr. McGillicuddy as he drug a ladder across the driveway.

"John McGillicuddy," she yelled back to him, "Be careful!"

Then she opened the door and entered the foyer.

"What in the world is that noise?"

She started up the stairs to check, but the sound of the horn honking again stopped her.

"The girls *are* in a hurry to go shopping," she said and, after taking one more glance up the stairs, quickly hurried to the foyer closet and grabbed her coat. She opened the front door. As it closed behind her, she was sure she heard more noises. She shook her head and mumbled, "What's going on around this place?" It was then she saw one of her sisters, Angie, staring at her through the open car window.

"Jane, you're starting to act like John. Are you talking to yourself?"

20

The Most Amazing Feat in His Life

"**T**here's no one in the house. This is our last chance. I'm going to need all of your help."

"*What do you want me to do, Bobby? I'll do whatever you say.*" It was Energizer.

"*Live up to your name, my powerful cousin. Give me the loudest cheers you've ever made. Encourage me so I'll really believe I can do this. I need the same from all of you.*"

And then, without another word, he went to work.

"*Puhrumba!*" He began to twist. "*Puhrumba!*" The twisting increased, and then one more, "*Puhrumba!*"

"*What are you doing?*" Aunt Glaring demanded. He was spinning almost out of control, and she saw him, from three pods away, launch himself into the air.

"*I'm going to save them,*" he shouted, as he guided himself toward the foot of the tall bed.

With tears still flowing down her face, his mom looked up at him. *"Bobby Bright! I've never seen you spin like this."*

She turned toward her children and the other bulbs and shouted, *"Cheer him as loudly as you can. Let him know you are with him."*

"Thanks, Mom," he could see the smile on her face as he looked down on the tree. And then he heard the cheers from the bulbs, which were loud and continuous.

This wasn't the first time he had flown. He had done so last year when he had saved the entire Bright family. And he had managed to do it just months ago when he had helped save Mrs. McGillicuddy. But this was, without question, his greatest test ever.

Even moments ago, when he had ejected himself from the pod and soared into the air, he wasn't completely confident the plan would work. But now, after hearing the cheers below, it was as if he had been injected with even more power.

"This is going to work," he shouted. *"Watch me, Mom!"* he yelled, and then he sailed high enough to reach the top of one of the four poles that sat at the corners of the bed.

"I'm going for the ceiling everyone." As soon as he said it, the bulbs cheered even louder. It was the most noise he had ever heard. Bobby felt his energy increase, and as he reached the ceiling, he turned in an arc and went into a steep dive. He was overcome with such power that he felt like he was suspended in a time warp.

It was two years ago. Mrs. McGillicuddy was speaking with Remington in the big room downstairs. She told him, "There is a time in everyone's life, Remington, when they experience a very special event that stands out above all other things they have ever done, or ever will do. When it happens, it will never be forgotten."

Now Bobby knew it must be true for bulbs too because he would never forget this moment.

"Puhrumba! Schnettz!" He repeated the words two more times and dove toward the bed. Now he could only hope his plan would work.

He knew his dad would be first, and as he approached, he saw him staring upward in disbelief.

Mr. McGillicuddy had just handed the man another strand of small white lights and was watching him attach the cord to the roof above the front door.

Mr. McGillicuddy's job was simple. Hold the ladder so it won't fall and occasionally hand him a strand of lights.

The ladder was sitting right in front of the glass door. He was on the third step, and after he handed the worker some bulbs, he carefully descended to the ground. As he stepped back from the ladder, he thought he heard noises coming from the house.

"Do you hear that noise?" Mr. McGillicuddy looked up toward the top of the ladder.

"All I hear is the wind. I'm coming down, so get ready to move the ladder over to the side of the porch."

He was upside down flying as fast as he could. A moment before he reached the bulbs, he arced upward. Looking like a helicopter preparing to land, Bobby spun in place and yelled the loudest, *Puhrumba* anyone ever heard.

The bulbs watched in absolute astonishment, and Bobby's mom shrieked loudly, "*Oh, no!*"

She saw her husband suddenly lifted into the air by the force of the spin. Both of them were suspended in the air for at least two seconds. Then she saw them move sideways.

Bobby was twirling so fast that his dad was caught in the draft, and because he wasn't spinning, he could be controlled for the landing.

Bobby began to reduce the force of his spin and felt the draft begin to weaken. He saw his dad start to drop, so he increased the spin slightly. They were still too far from the branches below. Increase, decrease, increase, decrease. The change of speed continued, until finally, Bobby was closer, and his dad hung suspended above the branch where his mom looked up with an astonished expression on her face.

Bobby reduced the suction of the mystical air draft a final time and shouted, "*Schnettz!*"

His dad dropped on to the branch, and the bulbs cheered wildly.

He wanted to spin in place and enjoy the moment and applause, but there was too much more to do. The job was only partially done. He had no time to savor the shouts of encouragement, although he definitely gained more power from the enthusiasm.

This time, he did not fly to the ceiling. As he left the tree, he guided himself only to the top of one of the bed posts before turning in an arc and speeding toward the bed cover where Whitening lay staring upward with a shocked look.

He then repeated the powerful suction he had produced for his dad less than a minute earlier.

They had just moved the ladder to the side of the tiny porch, and half of it blocked the front door. The worker was again stapling lights to the edge of the roof. In between the ZAP of the stapler, Mr. McGillicuddy was certain he heard those same noises again.

"Surely Jane didn't leave the television turned on."

"What did you say?" the man hollered from above.

"Nothing," Mr. McGillicuddy said, as he reached around the ladder. Holding it with his left hand, he tried to open the front glass door with his right hand.

It moved only a few inches before it hit the back part of the ladder, which started to shake.

"What the heck are you doing down there, McGilli-cuddy?" the man hollered. "Trying to break my neck?"

"Uh, sorry," Mr. McGillicuddy said.

As he moved the door away from the ladder and closed it, he heard noises again. "It sounds like cheering!"

"Are you talking to yourself?" the worker laughed, and looked down at the face of a very confused John McGillicuddy.

Whitening was on the tree. She lay next to Bobby's dad and they both had smiles on their faces.

Bobby just wished he had time to smile, but there was so much left to do. He had been successful to this point, but Mr. McGillicuddy might wander back into the room at any time.

He had to hurry because the hardest part was still ahead. The two bulbs, which Mrs. McGillicuddy got out of the drawer, had to be placed in the pods where his dad and Whitening had lived.

He put himself in reverse one more time and started flying upward. As he did, he noticed for the first time he was losing some of his energy.

"*You better hurry, Bobby,*" bellowed Uncle Flicker. "*I thought I heard that front door open downstairs. Somebody might be coming back in the house.*"

Bobby knew Mrs. McGillicuddy had left to go shopping with her sisters. He knew Mr. McGillicuddy was outside hanging lights on the roof. What he didn't know was how long it would take.

Bobby was above the bedpost when he heard his mother from below. "*What's wrong with you, Bobby? What are you doing?*"

He realized he had been suspended in the air, lost in thought.

"*I'm almost ready,*" he said in a loud voice, as he looked down at his mom and the other bulbs.

She looked up at him and saw him quickly turn into a nosedive, sweep down to the top of the bed cover, and then spin upward. The hard rotation produced the suction that picked up the first of the two replacement bulbs.

This is going to be the toughest part," he muttered to himself, as he moved sideways through the air and repeated what he had done earlier.

The bulb was dropped gently onto the branch where the empty pod sat next to his mom.

"Why are you putting it here?" his mom cried out.

"You'll see. Just give me a few more minutes."

He then sailed away from the tree, and headed skyward for one last dive. The bulbs were so amazed with Bobby's sensational feats that the cheering had stopped. They watched in silence.

"Come on!" He shouted. "Let me hear some noise. This is the most difficult part coming up."

"You got to be kidding me, Bobby." It was Energizer. "Everything you've done has been a miracle. How can anything be harder?"

"Just watch, Cousin, and keep your filaments crossed. I'm going to need some big time luck if this works."

The cheers started to ring out once more. Bobby turned and began a final dive to the bed. He repeated his earlier actions, and within five seconds, the last bulb had been sucked into the draft and moved to the side of the tree.

Now came the toughest part. The branch that held Whitening's pod was very small. There were no branches beneath it for support. If touched, it would bend downward. Anything not attached to the limb would fall to the floor. There had to be support for the branch or a way to tilt it upward if Bobby's plan was to work.

He increased and decreased the speed of the revolutions one more time and lowered the bulb. It seemed like it was taking forever, but he had to be certain the tip end of the bulb was guided toward the open pod.

Bobby looked down at Uncle Glimmer and his cousin Flash. *"I need your help."*

"What can we do?" whined Flash.

"You can do the biggest thing you've ever done," Bobby shouted. *"Both of you start shaking and lean forward and press up on the branch above you. I know it's not easy, but try to do it and keep doing it until I tell you to stop."*

"You must be kidding me, Bobby."

"Just do it, Flash," Uncle Glimmer ordered, and he began to shake vigorously. Flash looked at him, he looked up at Bobby, and then he started shaking.

"Harder, Flash! Shake harder!"

The flimsy branch, due to the shaking and the pressure from two nearby branches, bent partially backwards and the open end of the pod was now pointing in the air.

Bobby immediately maneuvered the end of the bulb against the pod and then, in what later would be called the most stupendous deed he ever did, Bobby yelled, *"Puhrumba! Puhrumba! Puhrumba! Puhrumba! Puhrumba!"*

The draft of air created by the gyrations was unbelievable.

He pushed the tip of the bulb inside the pod and shouted, *"Schnettz! Schnettz! Schnettz!"*

One second after he said Schnettz for a third time, the bulb made seven rapid rotations and locked itself into the pod.

Bobby diminished the rotary motion, and in what for him was now just a lazy spin, looked down at what he accomplished.

Then he heard the voices from below. Glimmer and Flash were telling the bulbs that couldn't see what had happened. And then, they all cheered his name.

With a big grin on his face, he tilted himself forward in mid-air and bowed to his family below. He had pulled it off, and managed to screw in the replacement bulb. Now he had to put the other bulb in his dad's pod.

No time to relax, he thought, but as he started to increase the rotation of his body he felt the power suddenly decrease. With one last weak *"Puhrumba"! He* lowered himself to the branch where his mom and dad waited.

He was very tired but when he heard the noise from downstairs, he realized he had no choice. Exhausted or not, he had to find a way to complete his plan.

21

Finishing Touches to Bobby's Plan

"Thanks again, Bennie," Mr. McGillicuddy said and closed the glass door behind him. He stood in the foyer for a moment and watched the truck pull out of the driveway.

The lights on the house had tested out okay and so had the lights on the three ornamental deer under the maple tree next to the mailbox at the street curb.

"Well, time to put those two new bulbs on the tree." He stepped onto the stairwell landing, but then he changed his mind.

"Maybe some of that yummy eggnog will get me more excited about those bulbs."

He turned and walked slowly toward the kitchen.

Bobby heard Mr. McGillicuddy below. *Saved by the eggnog*, he thought. He had rested for less than two minutes. It wasn't enough time to re-energize all of his power, but he had to do something.

"Mom, you and Aunt Glaring have got to do something special."

"What can we do?"

"I need for you to do just what Uncle Glimmer and Flash did a few minutes ago. You have to shake like they did, but you've got to lean backwards and try to pull the branch into the air. Then, hopefully, I'll be able to spin that bulb into the pod. So, let's go!"

Bobby quietly chanted, "Puhrumba! Puhrumba! Puhrumba!" He tried to lift himself into the air, but nothing happened.

Bobby's mom and aunt were shaking. He could feel the branch moving, but he wondered why he wasn't moving.

He was so weak he couldn't lift upward. If he was going to do this one more time, then he had to take a chance.

Shouting *"Puhrumba! Puhrumba! Puhrumba!"* as loudly as he could, Bobby moved only slightly. He felt as if he would fall back onto the branch, or even worse, clear to the floor.

But then, just as he thought there was no power left, he started to move upward once more. He quickly rotated as he gained altitude and in less than five seconds was even with the top of the bedpost.

He turned and nose-dived toward the bed. When he neared the front of it, he spun upward and created the necessary draft. The replacement bulb began to move into the suction created by the spinning, and now it was in the air. From below, Bobby saw his mom and aunt. It looked to him like they were shaking as hard as they could. With the little energy he had left, he shouted, *"Lean back! Lean back! Lean back!"*

Almost immediately he saw the branch bend back just enough so the pod was sticking slightly in the air. He maneuvered the bulb close to the tree and repeated his chant. *"Puhrumba! Puhrumba! Puhrumba! Puhrumba! Puhrumba!"*

The draft of air created by the gyrating increased and he was twirling almost as fast as the last time. He was again able to move the tip of the replacement bulb toward the pod, and as he did, he chanted, "*Schnettz! Schnettz! Schnettz!*"

The bulb rotated seven times and locked itself into the pod. Bobby wanted every bulb to cheer and enjoy the moment. But he knew better. "*Don't cheer. Don't say anything,*" he ordered. "*Let's not give Mr. McGillicuddy any reason to think something is happening in this room.*"

"*You are absolutely amazing, my son.*" It was his dad's first words since being placed on the tree.

He still wasn't completely safe, because he could still be seen, but for the moment there was nothing else Bobby could do for him.

Nearly out of power, Bobby softly said, "*Puhrumba,*" before barely spinning into his own pod.

Mr. McGillicuddy had just taken a seat at the kitchenette counter. It felt good to sit and relax. He took a couple of sips of eggnog and then hesitated when he thought he heard a noise again from upstairs.

He waited, but when he heard nothing else, he drained the cup dry with one big swallow. He got up to pour some more, and it was then he was certain he heard something that sounded like cheering.

"Enough is enough! I've got to find out what's going on. Jane must have left the TV set on."

He took one more swallow of eggnog from the newly filled mug and savored that great apple cinnamon taste.

"Boy! That is good. Jane sure knows how to make eggnog." He took another long swig of the creamy drink, licked his lips, and then with cup in hand, he left the kitchen.

Bobby knew Mr. McGillicuddy would be coming upstairs at any minute. Since he could still see the broken part of his dad's head, he knew the McGillicuddys would be able to see the same thing. He had to be hidden.

"Aunt Glaring, you have to help me. I'm exhausted. I can barely talk."

"I know, Bobby," she said. "I will help you."

"You don't even know what I need. Do you read minds?"

"Don't get too sassy, Nephew," she raised her voice slightly. "I am no dummy. I see my brother partially out in the open. So you just relax, and I'll take care of this."

Before Bobby could say or do anything, he felt the branch he was on and the one next to him begin to shake.

"What are you doing?"

But his aunt didn't answer. She just shook violently and then in her squeaky voice shouted, "Puhrumba!"

Bobby looked in amazement as the branch she was on lifted into the air, and then fell over the top of his dad. He and the branch were covered. Bobby peered around his mom, but couldn't see his dad.

"How did you do that, Aunt Glaring?"

"Just remember, Bobby, you are the most amazing and wonderful Christmas bulb in the world, but you are not the only one who can do magical things."

"Oh my gosh!" he gulped. "Do you have my powers?"

"No, no one will ever have the kind of power you have Bobby. But you should never forget that there is no one that can do everything on their own. There are times in all of our lives when we must ask for help from others, and there is nothing ever wrong with doing that."

"Oh, Glaring!" his mom interrupted, "You're such a wonderful sister-in-law. Thank you so much. He's hidden. I can't even see him."

And neither could Mr. McGillicuddy.

He entered the guest room. In the opposite corner sat the television set. It was turned off and there was no noise in the room.

"Man alive, I could have sworn I heard a sound from that TV set."

He looked around the room and then turned and stared at the tree. "Were you 'miracle' bulbs making all that noise I heard?"

He thought it was funny, and since there wasn't anyone there to enjoy his joke, he laughed at it himself.

Then he turned to reach for the two bulbs Mrs. McGillicuddy had put on the bed but didn't see them.

"Well, where are they? I saw them right there," he continued to mumble to himself. "I know they were there. I saw Jane put them there."

He leaned down and ran his hands over and under the folded cover on top of the bed. When he couldn't find either the red bulb or the green bulb that he was expecting to find, he picked up the cover and shook it. Nothing came loose. There were no bulbs.

So, he walked to the far side of the bed, ran his hands under the pillows, and made sure the bulbs weren't beneath them. Then, he checked the floor before returning to the tree.

At the front of the tree on the table was the white fluffy tree skirt. It looked like fallen snow. Mr. McGillicuddy reached down and lifted up a corner of the skirt to see if the bulbs were there, but still he found nothing.

"They have to be somewhere," he mumbled. "They didn't just fly into the air and disappear," he said in a louder voice. He searched the room with his eyes for a third time and shouted, "Where are you little bulbs hiding?"

He stood there for a moment, and then lifted up the opposite side of the skirt cover. When he did, he tipped the tree slightly to the right. For the briefest moment, it appeared it would fall off the table, but he was able to grab it quickly and set it upright.

"Where else could they be? Maybe she put them back in the drawer."

He smiled, and once more his eyes searched the room. "She must have put them back in the drawer."

As he turned and walked toward the dresser, he caught a glimpse of one of the front branches. It was crossed with another branch, and the part of the strand lying on top of it was slightly twisted.

He realized this was the spot where the broken bulb had been when Mrs. McGillicuddy had unscrewed it and placed it on the bed. *This should be empty*, he thought.

"How did this red bulb get here? This is so weird." He reached down and gently put his thumb and index finger around the bulb. He tried to move it, but it was already firmly screwed in.

"This is mind boggling. I know this was empty when I left the room." Then he looked to the left side of the tree and saw a green bulb where the chipped bulb had been.

"What is going on here? I am not crazy." He walked over to the dresser, picked up his cup of eggnog, and took a long swallow.

"I am so confused," he muttered to himself. "Get a hold of yourself, McGillicuddy."

He shook his head. He closed his eyes. He rubbed his eyelids. He emptied his cup. He put his cup down. He stretched his arms. He yawned. He took five determined steps to the tree, bent over, and examined the bulb on the side branch.

Nothing had changed from moments earlier. The bulb was still green and it looked new. He walked two steps to his right and bent over again. This time, he looked at the spot on the front of the tree where the other broken bulb had once been. He wasn't imagining things. There in its place was definitely a shiny new red bulb.

As he stood looking in amazement at the tree, he heard the voices of his wife and sisters-in-law.

"Where are the broken bulbs? How am I going to explain this?" he said loudly.

"I'm home, John. Is that you talking to yourself again?" She shouted up the stairs. He heard her two sisters laugh.

But John McGillicuddy was not laughing. He could not understand what had happened, but he sure wasn't going to tell his wife, or anyone else, about it.

22

Mr. McGillicuddy and his Miracle Bulbs

He looked at the tree one more time, shook his head, and started to leave, when he heard Mrs. McGillicuddy and her sisters tromping up the stairs.

"John, scoot out of the way so the girls can see the tree," Mrs. McGillicuddy said as the three waltzed into the room.

Mr. McGillicuddy did as he was told but moved only a couple of steps away. Standing close to the tree, he blocked the view of the lone green bulb at the side of the tree.

He wasn't sure why he was trying to cover it up since the other new one, laying in front, was still easy to see.

"Oh, this tree is even nicer than last year, Jane," said Angie, in her normal bubbly voice.

"It is nice," said Stacey. "Did you get a bigger table? This one is larger than last year, isn't it?"

Mrs. McGillicuddy answered, "No, same old table. But you are right, Stacey, it is a larger tree. We might need an extra set of lights and a few more ornaments on it.

"Well, plug it in. Let's see how it looks with the lights on," Angie said.

"Be my guest, Angie," Mr. McGillicuddy said, "Just flip the switch on the wall."

She did, and then the "oohing" and "aahing" started. "Just lovely. They're absolutely beautiful. Are these the same bulbs that were on this tree last Christmas? They were the brightest bulbs I had ever seen."

"Oh, who knows, Stacey," Mrs. McGillicuddy said. "You know, when John spilled all those lights after Christmas last year, we couldn't know for certain which strand had been on this tree. Plus, we lost three or four more strands because of the tornado."

"Well, they are beautiful."

Mrs. McGillicuddy stepped all the way back to the window and stood there for a moment staring at the front of the tree. "Yes, they are, Angie. Thank you, John, for putting the new bulbs on the tree."

"So, is this one of the new strands?" Angie asked.

"No, this is an old set. John just replaced two broken bulbs, which he had refused to remove. If you can believe it, he wanted to keep them for sentimental sake."

Stacey laughed and said, "Why John? Are they part of the family?"

"Well, don't get too smart with me, Stacey," Mr. McGillicuddy suddenly got brave and raised his voice. "These are the bulbs that saved your sister's life."

"Really!" Stacey looked at her sister. "These are the ones they found on your leg?"

"Yes, in fact," Mrs. McGillicuddy started laughing, "I'm getting as crazy as John. I even call them our 'miracle' bulbs. But enough of this, let's go!"

She playfully pushed Stacey out the door, and as she did, said, "Did you throw the broken bulbs away, John?"

"I've taken care of things, Jane," he said, but no one heard him because the three sisters were too busy chattering as they walked down the stairs.

Mr. McGillicuddy stood in the doorway listening until they had walked to the back of the house.

Then he started another conversation with himself. "This is so cotton-picking confusing. How did those bulbs get on the tree and where are the broken ones?"

Once more he bent over to take a closer look, and he touched some of the bulbs, moving them back and forth. He didn't see anything strange until he tried to separate a branch at the front of the tree which was crossed over the top of another one.

"My gosh!" He exclaimed. "That looks like one of the broken bulbs," and he started to pull the branches farther apart when he heard her voice.

"John! Quit talking to yourself up there," she shouted from below, "and come tell the girls goodbye."

He would check this out later. "Okay, I'm coming."

Bobby heard the women's voices at the front door, but he still just spoke loud enough to be heard. *"Uncle Flicker, I need your help. I'm in a big hurry and we are all in trouble if we don't get my dad hidden.*

"He is lying just beneath me under the branch Aunt Glaring moved. Can you see him, Uncle Flicker?"

"I'm trying," came the booming voice.

"How about you, Aunt Shining? Any chance you can see him?"

"I'm looking, but I don't see anyone but Dazzling."

"Dazzling, can you see my dad?"

"He's right where the branch starts to bend downward," she said. "I'm afraid he might fall."

"Dad, are you hearing all of this?"

"Yeah, just waiting my turn."

"Dad! I love you but sometimes you are too laid back. Come on, this is important. We need to hide you somewhere else."

"Bobby, maybe it's best we give it up. Maybe it's time for me to be thrown away."

"No! No!" His mom cried out.

"Calm down, Mom" Bobby said, and leaned to his left and touched her.

"Is he crazy?" she said.

"You know I don't want to leave any of you," Bobby's dad continued, "but this isn't a big tree. It will be tough to hide me."

From beneath them came Dazzling's voice again. "I can solve the problem if you will just let me, Robert."

"Dazzling, this is no time to be your snooty self. Don't try to get me upset."

"Okay, 'Bobby.' I will call you 'Bobby' so you will feel better, but I am going to solve the problem for my dear uncle."

"Let her help, if she can," Bobby's mom interrupted.

"He's right above me, Bobby. If you can get him loose, he will roll toward me, and if he bumps off of me, he has a big branch to fall on. I think Aunt Shining is right below me."

"Do you see the branch, Aunt Shining?"

"Yes, Bobby. I'm looking at it."

"They're right. He can roll down on it," Uncle Flicker's voice boomed from below.

"Okay, here's what we do. Bingo, you have to shake as hard as you can. Dad, you've got to shake too, and between the both of you shaking, you've got to get enough movement to start rolling toward Dazzling."

"I don't think I can shake that hard, Bobby," moaned Bingo. "Can't you just do your magic and pick him up and drop him where he has to go?"

"I'm too exhausted, Bingo. We all need to work together on this. I need your help. This is what family is all about. This time I can't do it all."

"I'm shaking, Bobby," his dad said in a louder voice, "You're right. It's time for me to change my attitude. I want to be with all of you, even if I'm hiding. Let's make this happen."

The bulbs all cheered, and Bingo shook harder.

Mrs. McGillicuddy was so tired after dinner that she headed directly to the bathroom to take a long warm bath. Her last words to Mr. McGillicuddy were, "Please, clean up the dishes and get the kitchen straightened up."

He fiddled around for nearly twenty minutes before he finally turned on the dishwasher. While he waited for the water to start running and the first cycle to begin, he thought he heard noises upstairs.

"Now what?" he grumbled. "Surely it's not the television set this time because I never turned it on. One thing for certain," he said as he continued to talk to himself, "I'm getting to the bottom of this right now."

He walked quickly through the kitchen, hall, and foyer and headed up the stairs.

"Quiet! Quiet!"

"What is it, Bobby?" asked Aunt Glaring.

"Stop the cheering. Can't you hear him coming?"

At that moment, Mr. McGillicuddy raced into the room, bent down abruptly, and stared at the front of the tree. Bobby knew he was staring right at him.

"Are you bulbs talking again? And you, Mr. blue bulb smack dab in the middle of the tree, I know there is something mysterious about you."

He stood there for a few seconds to catch his breath.

"What? No answer? No loud noises? Come on 'miracle' bulbs answer me!"

He waited again but after a few more seconds, shook his head and said, "Well, I know something is strange. Where is that broken bulb?"

He parted the front branches and looked at the spot where he had seen the bulb before dinner.

Then he moved the branches farther apart and looked at the branches near the trunk of the tree. He pulled some more branches apart. There was no broken bulb.

He bent down and looked on the table underneath the tree. "It must have fallen down here," he muttered.

But there was nothing. He remained bent over, head down, peering underneath the tree. "This is ridiculous."

When he pulled his head back and stood up, he screeched like he had seen a ghost. "Eeeekkk! Oh, my gosh!"

There stood Mrs. McGillicuddy, in her bathrobe, a shower cap still tied down over her hair, with a frown on her face.

"You scared me to death," he shouted.

She said nothing but backed to the hallway door. Then she pointed her finger toward the bed and said, "John, go sit down and tell me what is going on."

He brushed some tree needles off the front of his shirt, sat down on the edge of the bed, and said nothing.

"I'm waiting, John."

He stared at her, but still did not speak.

"John, I'm not going downstairs until you tell me what is going on. I get out of the bathtub, and I swear I hear the television on up here. I don't know why it would be, but I decide I better come up here and turn it off.

"So, I dry off and put my robe on. But by the time I get to the foot of the stairs, there is no television sound. When I reach the top of the stairs, I see you are not outdoors where you said you were going after you finished putting the dishes in the dishwasher. Instead, I find you talking to the Christmas tree and apparently looking for something.

"Would you like to tell me what is going on?"

He was still quiet and only stared into space.

She waited, and after about 15 seconds, sighed and said, "All right, it's been a long day for both of us. Maybe we are just too tired. Please turn the room light off when you leave."

Before she could turn around, he hopped up off of the bed and walked five steps to the doorway. He took his wife in his arms, and said, "I'm sorry. I just felt foolish about coming up here because I also thought I heard the television."

She started to respond, but he hurriedly added, "But I got everything taken care of, and I was just making sure all the bulbs were working."

She looked up at him as he held her, and said, "See, wasn't that easy to tell the truth?"

Then she laughed, and he laughed with her. They left the room together and were halfway down the stairs when she looked over her shoulder and said, "John, we forgot to turn off the lights."

"I'll get it," he said, and he walked back up the stairs and into the guest room.

He waited a few seconds until he knew she would be at the back of the house. "I know something is going on here," he said, as he looked at the bulbs on the tiny tree one more time. Then, he turned, and still muttering to himself, said, "But I'm not telling her. Why, she'd think I was really crazy.

23

Shine! Shine! It's Party Time Again

Bobby could feel his energy returning. After saving his dad and Whitening, it had felt good just to relax and do nothing.

He was sure Mr. McGillicuddy wouldn't say a word to his wife about the new bulbs or the missing ones. Everything was too confusing, but Bobby was also certain Mrs. McGillicuddy would throw the broken bulbs away if she found them.

During the last three days, Bobby and his family had spent time talking about the McGillicuddy's big Christmas party. Bobby had estimated it was about two weeks away and that Remington would be arriving in about three weeks.

But Bobby found out he was wrong.

The McGillicuddys reached the top of the stairs and talked outside the guest room. Mrs. McGillicuddy said, "Well, you've had your nap, John, so tell me about this marvelous new toilet paper toss game you've invented for the party."

Before he answered her, he reached his hand into the room and flipped the wall switch on. The brightness from the Christmas tree lights filled the room.

"They are beautiful," she said and stood in the doorway staring at the tree. Then she turned and walked back to the top of the stairs and said, "Okay, let's talk about your new game."

"You stand here at the top of the stairs," he said. "I'm going down below, and you are going to throw the rolls down toward that plate lying on the landing. Then I'll explain how we keep score."

"I can't believe I'm letting you do this," she said.

Minutes later Mr. McGillicuddy had persuaded her.

"Okay! That's it, John! We'll play this goofy game. I have to admit it is kind of fun, but I still can't believe I'm letting my guests throw toilet paper rolls at a plate. Can I change my mind in the next five days before the party, if I want?"

"Oh, Jane, it will be fun," Mr. McGillicuddy answered. "Everyone at the 'Big One' will like it."

When the McGillicuddy's had left and gone downstairs, Bobby yelled, *"Listen up! I've got good news. The big party is only five days away."*

"You mean, in less than a week we'll be entertaining," Flash said.

"I guess you could say that. When we shine, we do indeed entertain," said Bobby.

The McGillicuddy's Christmas party was always on a Sunday night in December, and it was filled with music, games, and lots of catered food. It was an evening their friends always looked forward to.

After all of the wonderful experiences from last year, it was a night Bobby and his family had anticipated eagerly. The fact it was being held earlier in the month made it even better, Bobby thought.

Earlier in the week, while the McGillicuddys were out shopping for last minute items for the party, he had made sure every bulb was in position to see as much of the room as possible. After briefly unscrewing himself from his pod, he had flown into the air and created a quick and efficient wind power draft. This allowed him to shuffle some of the bulbs located at the rear of the tree closer to the front.

Bobby's mom had been very proud of him.

He remembered her leaning over and tapping him on his forehead when he returned to his pod. "*That's a very sweet thing you did, Bobby. I'm glad you moved those bulbs into a better spot. It's very nice of you to be thinking of others, especially since you sit right here at the front.*"

Bobby's thoughts were suddenly interrupted.

The sound of the doorbell signaled what he had expected. It is party time.

Within a half hour, fifty guests were at the party. They came in small groups into the upstairs guest room as they waited to play games in the nearby rooms.

Just like last year, everyone who walked into the room had some kind of a comment about the brightly "shining" bulbs.

Every time someone said, "Will you look at how bright these bulbs are," they would *"turn up the juice,"* as Bobby liked to say, and shine even brighter.

"What are they saying?"

"Why are they pointing?"

"Look at the big face looking at me!"

The bulbs chattered away in "Bulbese" and Bobby joined them from time to time to interpret what the humans were saying.

"He just said he never saw such bright lights in his life."

"That's what you said people were saying last year, Bobby."

"Well, Sparkle, I think a lot of these people still remember how sparkling we were last year."

"Oh, Bobby, you are so cute at times," she chuckled. *"What did that lady say, the one who just had her face*

stuck so close to me that I could see the wrinkles under her eyes?"

"She just said this was the prettiest little tree she had ever seen, and she told the other woman it was because the lights are so bright."

"Well," Sparkle said, "We really are making the room brighter. Look at all the people staring at us."

"Unbelievable, Cheryl," said the man whose face was suddenly staring right at Bobby. "I'm telling you, I just saw that bulb and some of the other ones twist and move."

"That does it!" the woman yelled. "We'll play that silly game after you get some food in you."

And Bobby watched as the woman grabbed the man and pulled him to the doorway and out of the room.

Just as she did, the voice of Mr. McGillicuddy echoed up the stairs. "The dinner buffet is ready to be served."

"What's happening, Bobby?" his mom asked.

"It's time for everyone to eat," he answered. "Do you remember our own little party last year?"

Many of the bulbs answered, "Yes, we do!"

"How could we ever forget?" said Twinkle. "Does that mean we're ready to sing?"

Bobby replied, "Of course!"

And after the cheering stopped, the singing began.

> We're gonna shine all Christmas season,
> We're gonna shine every night.
> We're gonna shine, shine, shine,
> And be very, very bright.

And that's exactly what happened for the rest of the evening, until the final guest left just before 11 o'clock.

Mr. McGillicuddy wandered upstairs and walked into the guest room. "You did a good job tonight, 'miracle' bulbs. People talked about how bright you were all night long. After hearing the story about Jane and the tornado, some of them think you really are magical.

Why, that crazy old Doug Jones, who believes anything, told his wife you were twisting and turning on the tree.

"Of course, I've thought a couple of times you were twisting and turning too," and he laughed to himself. "I suppose you deserve a good night's sleep after working so hard."

Mr.McGillicuddy chuckled one more time, and then felt a chill run through the upper part of his body. He crossed his arms and hugged himself. "I get the strangest feeling around these bulbs."

"What's so funny, John?" Mrs. McGillicuddy called from downstairs.

"Oh just checking on your 'miracle' bulbs. They look tired. They must have worked too much tonight." Then he started laughing so hard he had to stop and catch his breath.

Mrs. McGillicuddy entered the room.

"Are you all right?"

"Of course, just joking about our special bulbs. They look tired after shining so brightly."

"That's it. Get down the stairs and into bed. We'll clean up tomorrow."

24

Surprising News

For nearly two weeks after the excitement of the big party, Bobby and his family remained dark. It was such a disappointment, not being able to shine for anyone. There were a couple of nights when the bulbs were on while Mr. McGillicuddy was working in his nearby upstairs office.

But otherwise, it was darkness for the Bright family.

"Why can't we be like the bulbs on the tree downstairs?" His mom asked the question nearly every day.

Bobby's answer was always the same. *"Mom, just think back to how bad it was for nine years, hidden at the back of the big tree. Sure, we were turned on every night, but nobody ever saw us. At least these last two years the people at the party saw us. And the most important thing is, it won't be long before Remington gets here. Then, we can shine for him for at least three days".*

But Bobby was wrong, and this time he was glad he was.

It was the morning of December 19th, and Mrs. McGillicuddy and her sister were visiting as they looked through the chest of drawers in the upstairs guest room. There was a special blanket that Angie wanted to borrow.

"I am so excited, Angie."

"Well, you should be," giggled her sister.

"You know, we have seen them every summer until this year. But with me hobbling around on a cane, and the house taking so long to repair after the tornado, we just couldn't visit."

"My gosh, Jane, that's the first time since Remington was born, isn't it?"

"Exactly. I've seen him every summer since he was a baby, until this year."

"So, when did you find out?"

"About an hour before you came over. Lisa called and said she had some great news."

"So when do they get here?"

"Come on," Mrs. McGillicuddy said, "let's go back downstairs. I think I remember that blanket is in our bedroom closet. I have some fresh eggnog in the refrigerator. We can have some, and I'll give you all the details."

"You mean John hasn't drunk all of it?"

"Not yet. I hid it in the fridge behind the prune juice."

"Well," Angie said, "then that's the only reason there is some left."

They both laughed.

"So, Remington, Lisa, and Richard will be here tomorrow for sure?" Angie asked.

"Yep! Lisa said that since we didn't spend any time together this summer, would we care if they left today and got here tomorrow evening."

As they walked out of the room, Angie said, "I bet that was an easy answer."

"Oh, yes. A whole week with Remington and my kids."

"*Oh my gosh!*" He waited until he was sure the two sisters were at the back of the house.

"*What is it, Bobby?*"

"*Is it good news or bad news?*"

"*Listen up, everyone!*" Bobby loved being the only bulb that understood human language. That meant he could translate good news. Of course, sometimes when it was bad news, it wasn't fun.

"*This is great news. Remington is coming early,*" he exclaimed.

"*When, when, when?*" The questions came from throughout the tree.

When Bobby told them, all of the bulbs cheered.

25

Remington is Here

Mr. and Mrs. McGillicuddy were working in the upstairs office. She answered the phone three times before noon, but none of them were about Remington's arrival.

Bobby remembered hearing Remington tell Mr. McGillicuddy last year that the trip from his house was more than 1,000 miles. Mrs. McGillicuddy had said earlier in the day it would probably be after 8 o'clock before Remington arrived.

However, Bobby and the McGillicuddys got a surprise much earlier. At 4:16 in the afternoon, the telephone call came. Bobby saw the face of the clock when he heard the phone ring. Mr. McGillicuddy was still working upstairs, and Mrs. McGillicuddy answered the phone downstairs.

It was less than a minute before Bobby heard her voice.

"Get down here quick! It's the kids, and they are only thirty minutes away. I want you to help me with some things."

Bobby heard Mr. McGillicuddy push the chair away from his desk. He could see through the doorway, and it was only a moment before Mr. McGillicuddy walked by and disappeared down the stairs.

But then he suddenly popped back into view. Bobby watched him as he walked into the guest room. He looked at the tree, and Bobby was certain he was looking directly at him.

"Well, you little 'miracle' bulbs, you better get warmed up." Mr. McGillicuddy laughed and turned on the wall switch. "You better shine your very best for Remington, or I might just throw you away." He laughed and left the room.

Less than a minute later, Bobby heard the familiar voice when the front door opened downstairs. "Surprise!"

"Oh, no!" Mrs. McGillicuddy shouted and she ran from the kitchen to the foyer. There he stood, her only grandchild, Remington McGillicuddy. She raced to him and picked him up.

They threw their arms around each other and hugged.

"My gosh, you eight-year-old handsome boy, you have gotten heavier. It's tougher to lift you than a year ago. Get down! You are too heavy to hold." She placed his feet on the floor and gave him another hug.

Remington started to ask her if she was surprised but never had the chance.

Rocket came racing into the foyer barking loudly. Right behind the dog was Mr. McGillicuddy.

Remington already had his arms stretched around the neck of Rocket. The big golden retriever was trying to lick Remington's cheeks.

"I haven't seen you in a year, Rocket," said Remington.

Before he could say anything else, Mrs. McGillicuddy said, "Remington McGillicuddy, you just tricked

Grandpa and me. Your mom said you would be here in 30 minutes."

"I know," he giggled, "we were in the driveway when Mom called you."

"Don't give away all your sugar, you little trickster," Mr. McGillicuddy said. He was standing between the dining room and foyer. "Come here to your grandpa. I heard what you just told Grandma. You played a trick on us."

At that moment, the door opened, and Remington's mom and dad came into the house. "Were you surprised?"

"Well, of course," Mrs. McGillicuddy said, "we were going to have your favorite apple cinnamon eggnog already poured in the mugs and waiting for you. And," she added, "some of your favorite cookies, Remington."

"It's okay, I can wait, Grandma. I've got something I want to do right now."

Remington pulled loose from Mrs. McGillicuddy and stepped up on the landing. He looked upstairs.

"What? You mean you don't want any cookies right now?"

Mrs. McGillicuddy laughed, and asked, "Are you sure he's feeling well, Lisa?"

Bobby heard the footsteps on the stairs.

"*Quiet! Start shining your very best.*"

"I hope my wonderful little Christmas tree is waiting for me. You told me it was even better than last year," Remington yelled down the stairs to his grandma, as he reached the top.

"Here I come, and I hope my buddies are in here."

"Your buddies? What buddies?"

"Oh, Mom, the bulbs, you know, those wonderful bulbs that winked at me last year. And my best bulb friend, Bobby."

"Remington," his mom yelled from downstairs, "I thought we had a talk about that."

"We did, and you said it was okay."

"No, I said it was okay to give a bulb a name, but not to think the bulb can talk."

"Okay, Mom!"

Remington ran into the room and squealed loudly. "Yeah! The lights are on. The bulbs are shining, and there you are, Bobby," he said and leaned down sticking his nose right up against the blue bulb on the front branch.

Then, he whispered quickly, "I know that's you, Bobby." He wanted to say more, but everyone walked into the room, including Rocket, who started barking as soon as he saw the lights shining on the tree. Then he suddenly growled. "Rocket, what's wrong with you?" Mr. McGillicuddy said. "We're all happy. Don't start growling."

Everyone laughed, and while his parents and grand-parents visited, Remington checked every bulb on the tree.

When Rocket growled at the tree again, everyone laughed some more.

"*Bobby Bright!*" his mom whispered to him.

With all the noise, Bobby could barely hear her. "*What, Mom?*"

"*Don't you play innocent with me, Bobby. Just because your father isn't nearby doesn't mean you can do what-*

ever you want. You know he would be angry at you if he saw what you just did."

"Oh, Mom! It wasn't that bad. I just winked at the dog."

"No, you winked about three times at him. We're lucky he didn't take a bite out of the front of the tree."

"Way to go, Bobby!" came the voice from the side of the tree.

"Energizer, you be quiet," Uncle Glimmer snapped at his son.

"And you be careful, Bobby Bright," his mom scolded.

Meanwhile, the laughter and conversation continued, and every bulb saw a freckled face staring at them up close.

It was a day to remember.

26

Don't Peek!

It was like last year, only better.

There were more hugs and kisses, and lots of questions and answers. When things became quieter, Mr. and Mrs. McGillicuddy started bringing out Christmas presents from the guest room closet.

Remington got excited and he wanted to help, but his grandfather said, "No, you just sit right there and watch, little guy."

Remington asked, "Why can't I help? You always tell me I should help bring the presents downstairs."

"Oh, you can bring them downstairs. In fact, start right now," Mrs. McGillicuddy said.

"But why can't I help take them out of the closet?"

"Because there is a monster in there," Mr. McGillicuddy said and laughed.

"There's no monster in there, Grandpa. Come on," Remington whined, "why can't I look inside the closet?"

"Because there is another big surprise in there, and it is not wrapped."

"Really, Grandma! You aren't kidding me?"

"Nope, I'm not kidding you, so stay out of there! Don't ruin a wonderful Christmas."

Eventually, everyone had their hands and arms full of presents, and they walked downstairs to the sports arena.

But as soon as all the presents were neatly placed around the tree, Remington hurried back upstairs, followed by Rocket who was barking loudly. They both slid through the doorway, and Rocket brushed the table as he came to a stop. The little tree shook for a moment and nearly tipped over. Remington told Rocket "Be careful and be quiet, right now!" Rocket stopped barking, and he and Remington sat there staring at the lights.

Remington looked directly at the dark blue bulb sitting at the front of the tree and thought back to the third day after Christmas last year. It was his final minutes in front of his special tree before he and his parents had left to return home.

He could still remember what he said. *"I'm going to miss you, my wonderful Christmas tree. I'm going to really miss my wonderful shining bulbs, and you, my very special blue bulb, I'm going to miss you the most."*

Remington sat there and stared. A tear rolled down his right cheek. He didn't want to cry, but he did. He couldn't understand why he liked this tree so much, but he was glad he did. He guessed it was because it was his very own tree.

"That means you are my very own bulbs too," Remington said. "I wish I didn't have to go, so I could be with you longer."

Then, as he sat there staring at the tree and the bulbs, the strangest thing happened. Remington was looking directly at the blue bulb in front when the bulb winked at him.

"I saw that! I saw you wink at me."

Remington heard his folks and grandparents at the foot of the stairs near the front door. He knew they were either going to call for him to come down and get in the car, or they were going to come upstairs and get him.

"Please, tell me! Do you have a name?"

Remington looked straight at the blue bulb. He hoped it would wink again, but it didn't. Then Remington heard them walking up the stairs. They were talking. He could hear his grandmother crying. She always cried when it was time for them to leave.

"Hurry, please tell me. Please! Pretty please!"

He heard the footsteps of his grandpa, and he turned to see him rounding the corner at the top of the stairs and only a few feet from the guest room doorway. "What's going on, Remington?"

Before Remington could answer, he heard a strange squeaky noise. When his granddad asked again, "What's going on?" Remington just stared at him in disbelief. "What is it, Remington?"

Remington answered, "Nothing," even though he was almost certain that he had just heard a squeaky noise that sounded like the name "Bobby."

The memory brought a smile to his face, and he looked straight at the blue bulb at the front of the tree. "I'm going to find out for sure this year. Your name is Bobby, isn't it?"

Remington waited, as if he thought he would hear an answer, but instead he got a bigger surprise. Suddenly Rocket started barking while running back and forth throughout the room, and Remington knew why. They both had just seen a Christmas tree light bulb winking at them.

27

Oh! What a Surprise!

Remington had spent most of his time in his room the last two days, since Bobby had shocked him by winking at him three times.

In fact, Remington spent so much time in the room that last night his dad shouted, "Get down here and visit with your grandparents."

When Remington had left, Bobby told the rest of the bulbs, *"Hey! It's okay. He's got to spend time with his family too."*

It was the morning of December 23rd. He had counted the presents under the big tree downstairs last night before he was sent to bed. Between the presents downstairs and the ones upstairs, there were close to forty gifts.

He had looked at the names on each one, and at least fifteen of the presents were his.

It wasn't the wrapped gifts that excited him but the mystery of the one in the closet that he was forbidden to touch or see. He thought he must have started to peek inside at least 200 different times in the past two days.

He knew he shouldn't, and so at 10:30 in the morning, just two days before Christmas, he was still being a good boy. Nevertheless, it wouldn't be long until the temptation would be too much to resist, and Christmas for Remington and his family, and for Bobby Bright and his family, would change dramatically.

"We are leaving, John," Mrs. McGillicuddy waved from the driver's seat of the SUV. "We're getting the rest of the food for tomorrow night and a couple of little stocking stuffers. Make sure you check on Remington in a few minutes and see if he's okay. He said he was going to play upstairs. You can't get him away from that tree."

She turned her head and looked in the backseat, "Do you think he heard a word I said, Lisa?"

"Who knows? He's just upset that you are making him go out and fix the lights on those three deer. He'd be happy to leave them unlit."

"Well, they are not going to be. Remington loves to go outside at night and see the lights on the deer and on the front of the house."

"I don't know, Mom," Remington's dad said, as the SUV left the driveway. "Remington doesn't think any lights are as important as the ones on his tree. I can't get over how he's so captivated by them."

"No doubt, it must be because they are 'miracle' bulbs."

"Oh, Mom!" Lisa started laughing at her mother-in-law. "Do you really believe what Dad says?"

"Lisa, I've heard it every week since the tornado. John claimed he saw them move before they were put up in the closet, after the house was repaired."

"Are you sure Dad is feeling okay, Mom?"

"Yes, your father-in-law is fine," she laughed. "Well, maybe most of the time."

"'Miracle' bulbs! Unbelievable," Richard said, and then the car turned the corner and pulled completely out of sight of the house. All three of them laughed.

Mr. McGillicuddy wasn't laughing.

He had already tested the small blinking bulbs on the deer statues that sat under the large tree. There was no blinking. In fact, there was no light.

Just minutes after the car had left the driveway, he had finished swapping the old power cord for a new one, which now stretched across the middle of the circular driveway and into the garage. But it had not solved the problem. The bulbs still did not light.

He wanted to go inside and not even mess with them anymore. It wasn't because he was cold. The weather was actually wonderful, especially for two days before Christmas. All he wanted to do was watch some football, relax and have a cup of that yummy eggnog.

But then he thought of Remington and how much he liked the lighted deer. So, he decided to try one more time.

At 10:45, Remington finally gave in. He decided he couldn't wait. Plus, no one had to know.

"I'll just take a quick peek. If it's in a box, I won't open it."

Then he laughed to himself. "I sound like Grandpa. I'm talking to myself."

He looked directly at his tree and chuckled, "Don't tell anybody, Bobby. I'm going to do it."

When Mr. McGillicuddy walked back to the garage, he noticed Mrs. McGillicuddy had not completely closed the door to the kitchen when she had left a few minutes earlier. It was slightly ajar. He walked inside and yelled, "Remington, are you okay?"

At first, there was no answer. He waited for a couple of seconds and then started to yell again. At that moment, he heard Remington's voice from upstairs.

"I'm okay, Grandpa. What are you doing?"

"I'm working on the deer trying to get them to light. Do you want to come help?"

"No, not now, I'm playing."

"Okay!" Mr. McGillicuddy yelled back and then mumbled, "Remington's probably talking to those bulbs."

He laughed and shut the door. It was something he later wished he hadn't done.

Remington was squealing for joy, jumping up and down, and running around the room. He almost bumped into the table and the tree. He couldn't believe what he had seen. All he wanted to do was fly or do something crazy.

"What a Christmas gift! I've got to celebrate," he yelled. He looked around the room one time, and then he climbed up on the bed and did what he had been told never to do.

The louder he screamed, the higher he bounced above the bedspread and the thick downy coverlet that lay on top.

Remington knew he shouldn't have opened the closet door, and he had almost changed his mind when his grandpa had yelled at him a couple of minutes earlier.

"Boy, am I glad I looked," he squealed. And then he jumped even higher. "I'm getting a computer for Christmas."

When he had first peeked inside the closet, he saw only clothes and suitcases. He decided to change his mind and close the door. However, a slight rush of air blew a large sheet of paper off one of the suitcases. Underneath it were two boxes.

The big picture on the side of the bottom box was all he needed to see. He squealed again as he thought about it.

"My very own computer," he shrieked.

And when he jumped as high as he could, the next shriek was not a happy one.

"*What's wrong with that kid?*" yelled Uncle Flicker from the middle of the tree.

"*Is he all right?*"

233

"What's going on?"

"Look at him!"

"That's one happy little boy!"

As the others jabbered amongst themselves, Bobby quickly told his mom and Aunt Glaring what Remington had just found. They started telling other bulbs, as Bobby's attention remained focused on Remington. He didn't like what he saw. Remington was jumping way too high in the air.

It was that thick, white cover on top of the bed that worried Bobby. As Remington came down on top of it, he nearly lost his balance, but then regained it almost immediately and jumped even higher.

"A computer, wow!" Remington shouted.

Bobby recalled overhearing Mr. McGillicuddy say that Remington wanted a small children's computer for Christmas, but he didn't think his mom and dad would buy him one.

So Bobby knew this was a huge surprise.

"Yippee!" Remington jumped as high as he could.

"He's going to get hurt," Bobby's mom yelled as she watched Remington sail higher in the air than before.

The other bulbs started shouting to Bobby.

"Make him stop, Bobby."

"He could get hurt. Can you make him stop, Bobby?"

But Bobby could do nothing, and then, as Remington let out another wild "Whoopee," all of the bulbs saw him stumble when his feet landed. "Ouch!" he cried, and he tumbled forward. He tried to grab one of the tall posters at the foot of the bed, but his hand missed it.

He crashed to the floor so hard that a loud thud echoed through the room as he fell forward and his nose smashed hard against the wooden floor.

Bobby felt the table and the tree shake slightly.

The bulbs looked in disbelief.

There was no sound, nor movement, from Remington.

Bobby could see the upper part of Remington's body. He was lying in the middle of the room.

His knees had hit the floor first before he had fallen forward on to his face. He had then rolled over and was lying partially on the Oriental rug at the foot of the bed. He lay on his left shoulder, and Bobby watched as blood trickled from Remington's nose.

There was no crying, no whimpering, and no movement.

28

Bobby Flies to the Rescue

After Mr. McGillicuddy checked on Remington, he had returned to the front yard and spent ten minutes checking power cords and switching old bulbs for new ones. Finally, he was able to get all of the lights to flash at the same time. Then he tested them one more time to be certain each blue and white bulb was glowing brightly.

Since Mrs. McGillicuddy, Lisa, and Richard had not yet returned from shopping, he decided to check the lights on the roof just above the garage. Last night he had noticed a couple of bulbs had burned out. The eggnog could wait just a little longer. Plus, he knew it would taste even better in a few minutes.

But just as he was about to get the ladder out of the garage, he remembered something he had forgotten to do.

"Oh, brother!" he said to himself. "I was supposed to wrap Remington's computer and put it under the tree. I better finish checking these lights and get inside and wrap that computer before I get in trouble with Jane."

Remington did not move. His nose was already swelling up and it had started to turn black and blue.

Every bulb was asking questions.

"Can we stop the bleeding like we did with Mrs. McGillicuddy?"

"Mom, we're attached to the tree. How could we get loose?"

"Of course, how stupid of me."

"But just because we can't get the strand free doesn't mean I can't get loose."

"Then do it!"

Bobby wasted no time. "Puhrumba! Puhrumba! Puhrumba!"

He tried to twist and unscrew himself from the pod, but nothing happened. For just an instant, he feared his magical powers might not be working, but then he yelled even louder, "*Schnettz! Schnettz! Schnettz!*"

Suddenly he was spinning and within two seconds had freed himself from the pod and was flying in the air.

When he was high above Remington, he decreased his power and spun toward the ground.

He gently landed on the rug next to Remington's head.

Bobby wasn't sure Remington was breathing and waited to see if there was any movement.

"*Do something!*" his brother Dimmer shouted from the tree.

Bobby said only one "*Puhrumba!*" and then rolled up against Remington's nose. Bobby knew he was hot and hoped he wouldn't burn Remington's face.

He felt the wetness of Remington's nose as he pressed against his face.

He lay still, and in a few seconds, he felt Remington's face slightly move. Then he heard a moan followed by a series of groans, which was followed by uncontrollable crying.

"*He's awake!*" one of the bulbs shouted.

"*That's the good news, but he is hurt bad,*" Bobby shouted back.

Remington started screaming and tried to wipe the tears and flecks of drying blood from his face.

"Isn't there anyone who can help him?" Bingo called out from the middle of the tree.

"Don't let him see you, Bobby," his mom yelled.

Bobby thought for the briefest of moments, what difference would it really make, but then, knowing his mother was right, he yelled, "Puhrumba!" and flew away from Remington and into the air where he hovered above him. He knew what he had to do.

"Bobby!" his mom shrieked just seconds later. "Where are you going?"

He had no time to answer, and his family watched him with amazement as he shouted, "Puhrumba! Puhrumba! Puhrumba! Schnettz! Schnettz! Schnettz!"

And then, just to make sure that the most amazing thing he had ever done would take place, he added, "Buhhhhroom!"

When he said that one word, the energy raced through his body, and he spun through the doorway with a tremendous force, barely seeing the shocked look on the faces of the other bulbs. Spinning faster than he had ever spun in his life, he flew down the staircase and sailed to the front door. He was rotating so fast he could barely see. To his left he heard the chandelier in the foyer shake and the small lights inside of it rattling against each other.

The more it shook, the louder the noise, and it didn't take but a few seconds before Rocket left the kitchen and came running toward the foyer with his big paws pounding on the floor. The dog barked louder than Bobby had ever heard.

He reduced the velocity of his spin and immediately saw the dog rise up on his back legs. His front paws stretched into the air, and he tried to touch Bobby. When Bobby started spinning faster, Rocket growled and barked even louder and then leaped into the air once more.

He knew his plan had a chance to work. First though, he must get Mr. McGillicuddy into the house. He was certain the way to do it was to create a lot of noise.

So Bobby spun as fast as he thought was possible, and the force of the air circulating through the room was enough to make Rocket even crazier. The dog jumped higher, and each time he landed, he would spin in a circle, looking like he was trying to catch his tail. As dangerous as the situation was, Bobby couldn't help but laugh. It was a funny sight.

But the fearful sounds from Remington upstairs, and his pleas for "someone, please help me" was anything but funny.

As he continued to circle in the air, Bobby knew he had to do more. Somehow, he had to get the door opened so they could be heard.

"Why can't you hear Rocket, Mr. McGillicuddy?" Bobby yelled.

And then, almost as if his question had been answered, an idea came to him that just might work. He began to fly through the foyer to the edge of the door and then back to the entrance of the living room. He did this at least four times, and no matter which way he flew, Rocket followed him back and forth.

Finally, he put the brakes on just before he touched the top of the front door. He continued to rotate there, and Rocket made a lunge for him. When the Golden Retriever did, he missed and hit the door.

Bobby repeated the entire trick again, flying to the other end of the foyer, and then racing back to the door. Each time he nearly hit the door, but managed to stop just in time.

But Rocket wasn't able to do so. Each time the dog crashed into the door.

It was exactly what Bobby wanted. Rocket was hitting the door and barking loudly. Plus, from upstairs came the shouts for help from Remington. Bobby yelled, *"How can you not hear this noise, Mr. McGillicuddy?"*

Mr. McGillicuddy was still on the top step of the ladder.

He had just replaced two burned out bulbs with new ones when he heard a loud THUMP that sounded like it came from near the front door.

"What was that?"

He stepped down two steps and reached for a hammer that lay in the drainpipe below the roof.

"Three more bulbs to change," he muttered to himself, "and I'm going inside and have some eggnog."

Stepping off the ladder, he clamped the sides together and started to carry it around the corner of the garage. However, he had taken only two steps when he heard the loud thump again and heard Rocket barking.

"What in the world is going on?"

He placed the ladder against the side of the house, and as he did, he heard a loud crash.

"That does it. I'm finding out what's going on." He ran to the porch and saw the front door shaking. Rocket sounded like he was imitating a wolf.

"What's going on boy?" Mr. McGillicuddy shouted.

When Rocket quit barking for a moment, Mr. McGillicuddy heard Remington.

"Oh my goodness! Remington, is that you?"

He threw open the glass door, and as he grabbed for the wooden door, something struck it from inside. Thump! He turned the handle and pushed open the door.

Now, he clearly heard Remington crying for help. A shiver went through his body, and he raced toward the stairs.

"I'm coming, Remington," he shouted, and for the briefest moment, he thought he saw something in the air.

Bobby heard Mr. McGillicuddy's voice and saw the door handle turn.

He had done it. Remington would be saved. Bobby turned in mid-air and flew up the stairwell. Over his shoulder, he saw Mr. McGillicuddy swing the door open. As Bobby reached the top of the stairs, he suddenly felt a loss of power and started to fall. He had just enough energy to turn to his left and glide into the room. His mom and Aunt Glaring watched him as he settled between them at the front of the tree.

Bobby was so exhausted he was unable to twist himself into his pod. As he lay there, he could see poor Remington. His swollen nose still had some specks of dry blood on it. Bobby was sure Remington was looking straight at him. He smiled and winked at the little guy on the floor. When he did, Remington stopped crying and slowly closed his eyes.

Mr. McGillicuddy ran up the stairs two at a time and slid around the corner. He could see Remington through the doorway, lying against the small piano-organ that sat against the far wall.

"Remington!" he yelled, and he sprinted into the room, dropping to both knees. He gently picked up Remington's head. The first thing he saw was the dried blood beneath his grandson's nose and a bad cut above his lip.

"Talk to me, Buddy, talk to Granddaddy. Oh, please, say something."

Tears were visible on Remington's cheeks, and because he had cried for so long, his lips and the bottom of his chin were soaked.

"Please, Remington, say something." Mr. McGillicuddy rolled him over on his back and attempted to sit him upward. When he did, Remington's head fell forward and there was the slightest groan.

"Thank God, at least there's a sound."

He leaned Remington against the side of the piano and that's when he saw the black and blue swollen right eye and the deep purple tint on his cheek.

"I've got to call Jane and the kids. Please, Remington, answer me. Can't you hear me?"

He laid Remington on his left side to protect the badly swollen right side of his face. Then he took the cell phone from his pocket and started to dial, but stopped almost immediately when he saw Remington's eyes slowly open and heard him start crying.

"Grandpa, is that you?"

"It's me, Buddy. You are going to be okay. Will you trust me?"

But, there was no answer. Just that quickly, Remington passed out and lost consciousness.

Mr. McGillicuddy knocked away flecks of caked blood that had dried on the fine strands of red hair on Remington's head. He reached down and gave his grandson a kiss, and then he began to cry. "What have I let happen to my buddy?" he said, and he sobbed loudly. For the second time he started to call his wife, but before he had completed dialing, he heard the noise that made him sigh with relief. The garage door was opening.

"Oh, thank heavens! They are back."

He leapt to his feet and ran from the room, shouting to the top of his voice, "Get in the house right now! Something terrible has happened."

29

A Christmas Eve Headache

"Remington, please tell me again. What happened? Are you really still not able to remember, or are you just trying to forget what you did?"

"What do you mean?" he asked, and moved so he could sit higher in the bed. Sitting next to him, his mom said, "Here, let me make you more comfortable," and she shifted the pillow so it would be directly behind his head. Part of the bandage wrapped around his skull was turned up near his right ear and she pulled it down to make sure it was straight and covered the area near his temple.

As she continued to look at her only son, she began to feel faint herself. Remington's head was still swollen. Just beneath the bottom edge of the bandage was a purplish color that circled his forehead, continued downward to his cheeks, and even to his chin, where he had first hit the floor.

He was definitely a lucky little boy, she thought. The medical personnel at the emergency room had explained that Remington was fortunate he didn't have a concussion. The hospital doctor, who finally examined Remington, had also pointed out to them that Mr. McGillicuddy had found him just in time. Had he not, Remington might have lost consciousness again and suffered more than just bruises and a sore head. All of them were aware this could have been a greater tragedy if Remington had been discovered a few minutes later.

Her thoughts were interrupted when she realized Remington was talking to her.

"Mom, I'm answering you. I am comfortable, thank you. I just want to be able to look at Bobby and all of my bulb friends."

"Oh, Remington! When are you going to quit believing those bulbs are for real?"

"I told you, Mom" said Remington, and pointed a finger at the blue bulb in the very front of the tree. That one right there," he added. "That's Bobby, the blue one.

"That's the bulb that saved me. He flew down the stairs and caused Rocket to bark so loudly that Grandpa heard him and came inside. Do you remember what Grandpa told you and dad when you were putting me in the car to go to the hospital?"

Remington's mom shook her head.

"He told you that he didn't come inside until he heard Rocket barking louder than he had ever heard him before."

"Well, you are right about that," Remington's mom said. "Your Grandpa said he heard something crashing against the door."

"See, told you," Remington said, and reached up and hugged his mom.

"Well, young man, you know if you would tell me exactly what happened when you fell, and not keep trying to say you aren't sure you remember, maybe I would believe you about your friend Bobby."

"Really!" he shrieked. "Really, Mom!"

"Well, maybe I would, but not about flying downstairs." she said.

But before Remington could say anything else, his grandma walked into the room. "It's almost noon. Are you ready for some lunch?" she asked, "And more importantly, how is my little, redheaded love bug feeling?"

Remington smiled and gave his grandma a hug as she bent down over the bed. "Better, I guess, Grandma, but my head still hurts."

"Well, it's going to hurt for sometime, according to the doctor. You are a very lucky boy, Remington. Do you remember everything he told you?"

"Most of it, I think," and he slightly nodded his head. "Ouch, that hurts!"

His mom asked, "What does?"

"Just when I turn my head too quickly."

"Well, then sit there and listen to me," Mrs. McGillicuddy interrupted. "We are very blessed that you are alive. Did you tell him everything, Lisa?"

"No, we had just made a deal that if he would tell me everything that happened, instead of acting like he doesn't really know, then I might believe him about that silly blue bulb."

"Remington, even more important than telling us everything that happened, is the fact you are a lucky boy. You know, if Grandpa had not found you, it's possible you would have gone into a coma. If that had happened then you wouldn't even be talking to us now. So you should feel very lucky."

"What's a coma, Grandma?"

"A coma is like a long sleep. Doctors can't wake you up. Some people stay that way for days, weeks, months, or even years."

"Oh my gosh! I owe you even more, my wonderful buddy," Remington said, and quickly threw the blanket off him. He slowly moved up and sat on his knees.

"Oh, Remington," his mom pleaded, "don't try to make us believe he saved your life."

"I told you he did, Mom, and now I'm going to tell all of you what happened."

"Well, if you mean it, I'm going to go get your daddy and grandpa so they can hear the real story." Mrs. McGillicuddy hurried out of the room and went downstairs.

They sat there saying nothing for a few seconds, and then his mom looked at Remington. "You better tell us the whole truth, or when you wake up tomorrow morning, there might not be any presents from Santa Claus, or us."

"Oh, Mom, you know that's not true. I'm getting Grandma and Grandpa's big gift. That's why I had the accident."

"What do you mean?"

"Well, should I tell you or wait for everyone?"

"What's going on, Remington?" his dad walked quickly into the room, followed by his parents.

"Just listen, Dad, but please don't spank me."

"Now, will you please tell us, Bobby?" Dimmer begged.

"Yes, tell us now. They are all busy downstairs singing," Uncle Flicker added, "So we've got plenty of time. Tell us exactly what they said and why everyone came over, touched you, and then laughed before they left the room."

"All right, here's the story," and Bobby again explained that the medical people, who arrived in the ambulance, had told Remington he was very fortunate he was not more seriously injured, and that later the doctors told him he had been very close to going into a coma.

"All right, we know all of that," bellowed Uncle Flicker in his deep voice. "Just tell us about tonight and why everyone was touching you."

"Take it easy. I'm getting to it. After everyone came into the room, Remington started explaining how he had peeked in the closet, when he knew he shouldn't, and how he had discovered his Christmas surprise."

"What was it again, Bobby?" Bingo interrupted.

"It was a junior computer. That's almost like a regular computer, but not with all of the fancy extras."

"What's a computer again?" It was Aunt Glaring.

"I've explained this twice before."

"I know, I just don't understand."

"Computers do everything in human life, Aunt Glaring. They make the world go around, according to Mr. McGillicuddy."

"Okay, so what else did he say?" she sighed. "And, I promise I won't interrupt anymore."

"He told them he got so excited, after he had looked in the closet and saw the computer boxes, that he started jumping up and down on the bed."

"Is that why his dad looked like he was going to spank him?" Bobby's mom asked.

"Yep, but Mrs. McGillicuddy told him to listen to Remington's story. Afterwards, they all admitted that when they were children they had peeked inside gifts when they shouldn't have. After that, everyone started hugging each other, and they told Remington they forgave him."

"But why did they come over and start touching you?" Sparkle asked her brother.

"Well, that's when Remington told them that he remembered nothing from the time he fell off of the bed, until he felt something hot. He said that was when he opened his eyes and saw me on his left cheek."

"They didn't believe his story, did they?" It was Uncle Flicker again.

"Of course they didn't believe him."

"Do you think they ever will?" Dazzling asked.

"Probably not, but here's the funny part. When Remington told them, Mr. McGillicuddy started coughing and acting strange. Did anyone notice?"

"I did," replied Aunt Glaring.

"Exactly. Mr. McGillicuddy thinks he saw me flying up the stairwell when he came into the house."

"What did he say?"

Bobby chuckled as he spoke, "He said, 'Don't be so sure Remington didn't see that,' and then Mrs. McGillicuddy said, 'John, are you out of your mind? Why would you say that?'"

"Did Remington say anything else?"

"Oh, yeah, Mom. He told them he definitely believed I had saved him. Did most of you see him come touch me when he said it?"

Bobby watched many of the bulbs near him nod back and forth.

"Well, that's when he told me 'thanks.'"

"It looked to me like all of the others said something."

"Very good, Aunt Glaring," Bobby smiled and said. *"They all looked at me and said, 'thanks,' but I don't think they believed it.*

"Do you think they will ever understand what a hero you are, Bobby, and what you have done for this family this year?"

It was Dimmer who asked the question, and Bobby could tell his brother was proud of him.

"Probably not. But remember, all of us are heroes, not just me."

"Well, let's hope they don't need anymore of your heroics," Dimmer added.

"I hope not," Bobby sighed. *"I need a rest."*

"Just have enough energy to shine brightly tonight, Bobby," his mom said. *"You know how much Remington will want to watch us on Christmas Eve."*

It was almost time for Christmas Eve dinner and then the traditional exchange of gifts. "Did you have a good nap, Remington?" his mom asked when she came into the room and saw him sitting on the edge of the bed with a big smile on his face.

"Yes, I've been awake a few minutes. Bobby just told me 'Hi'."

She shook her head in disbelief. "Remington, do you really believe that bulb has a name?"

"Oh, yeah, Mom. I should have told you earlier about him, just like I should have told you about peeking in the closet and seeing my computer. I was just afraid to say anything."

"What do you mean, Sweetheart?"

"Bobby said his name to me last year. He did it twice. Once was on the second day after Christmas. The other was when we were getting ready to go home."

"You're telling me this bulb spoke to you and told you his name was 'Bobby'?" She smiled, reached down, and kissed Remington on his right cheek.

"Yep, sort of."

"What kind of, sort of, do you mean?"

"Well, just before we left for home last year, I asked if he had a name, and I swear, Mom, I heard the word 'Bobby.' I promise you, Mom, that's what he said."

Before she could say anything, Remington grinned and said, "And he did it just a few minutes ago too. His name is Bobby, and I know he saved my life. You heard grandpa, Mom. He believes Bobby and all the bulbs helped save Grandma after she got hurt during the tornado."

"Oh, Remington, these are bulbs."

"Yep, Mom, but they are the most magical bulbs in the whole world."

His mom turned and stared at the tree. Remington watched her as she looked at the bright lights.

"You think I'm right, don't you, Mom? These are special bulbs."

"Well," she answered, "I guess if they did all that you and your granddaddy believe they did, then they must be special. But you had better enjoy them before we leave day after tomorrow. You do remember what we talked about, don't you?"

"I'm not sure. What did we talk about?"

"Not to say anything to your grandparents about next Christmas. We don't want to get them upset or spoil the surprise."

"Oh, Mom, that means I won't see Bobby next year."

"No you won't, little guy."

30

A Shocking Christmas Eve

The bulbs were lonely because Remington was not there to enjoy the lights. However, Bobby and his family understood. It was dinnertime on Christmas Eve, and downstairs Remington, and his parents and grandparents, were enjoying a wonderful meal prepared by Mrs. McGillicuddy. The dinner included many of her favorite recipes and the delicious food she loved to cook.

Bobby listened to the sounds of talking and laughter from the dining room table. But his thoughts were on what he had heard Remington say earlier in the day. *That means I won't see Bobby next year.*

As he continued to think about those words, he heard just enough of the conversation below to know that dessert was over and many different flavors of ice cream and three different pies had been eaten by the McGillicuddy family.

Now, they had left the dining room and gone further back in the house to unwrap the presents under the big Christmas tree. Bobby didn't understand everything that was said, but he certainly recognized the excited screech Remington made whenever he opened a gift. However, the loudest squeal came when Remington opened his final present, which was the new junior computer. Not even knowing what the gift was had taken away from the thrill of getting his very own computer.

After the gifts came the traditional singing of Christmas carols, and finally when it was time for bed, a quiet settled throughout the house. Within a few minutes, Bobby heard Remington coming up the stairs. He saw him enter the room, followed by his mom. He thought Remington looked very tired.

He watched as Remington's mother quickly helped him put his pajamas on. When Remington tried to pull the hockey jersey that he liked to sleep in over the top of his head, she had to help because the bandage was so thick.

"Mom, turn the tree lights on, please. You know I can't go to sleep without them on."

"Here, first take your medicine," she said, as Remington crawled into the bed and pulled the covers up around his neck.

"How long do I have to take these pills, Mom?"

"The doctor said you will need to take them for at least two weeks."

"Do I get some water with them?"

"Of course! Hold on, I'll be right back."

"Well, turn the tree lights on first."

His mom flipped the switch on the wall as she walked toward the nearby bathroom.

Bobby looked at Remington, who had the covers pulled clear up under his neck, a huge bandage on his head, his black and blue nose puffy and swollen, and a huge scab on the end of his chin where he had cut himself when he had fallen to the floor.

Bobby needed to make Remington smile, and the way to do it was to do something very special. He felt ornery, just like he had last year after Christmas.

"*Here I go,*" he whispered to himself. Then he quietly said, "*Puhrumba*" and that's when he winked and managed to squeal, "*I'm Bobby!*"

"Mom!" Remington yelled as loud as he could.

She heard him and nearly spilled the water in the glass as she ran through the doorway.

"What is it? Are you all right?"

Remington was more than all right. He looked better than he had since the accident. He was standing beside his bed with a huge grin on his face.

"I'm okay, Mom, just a little dizzy."

"Get back in bed," she said as she placed the glass on the nearby window seat. Then she put her arms around him.

"I'll be fine," and he pulled loose from her and walked to the tree. He stood looking at the blue bulb in front.

"I heard him, Mom. I really did. He said 'I'm Bobby,' and it really was his voice coming from the tree."

She sat down in the straight-backed chair, which was in front of the window, and watched her son in disbelief. It was one thing to have an imaginary friend. She remembered her imaginary friend named Ginny, who she talked to from the time she was three years old until she was almost eight.

Surely this must be Remington's imaginary friend, and yet, the way he talked about that blue bulb was different.

"Mom! Hello, Mom! Earth to Mom!"

She realized she had been staring at Remington but not listening while he had been talking to her.

He started to walk toward his mother, and then suddenly he grabbed for one of the posters at the end of the bed.

"What's wrong, Remington?" She jumped up and reached for him.

"I really feel dizzy," he replied.

"Get back in bed right now!"

She whispered into his ear, "Bobby Bright, you are going to get us in trouble!"

"Oh, Mom, you worry too much. He doesn't understand 'Bulbese,' but he does understand the word 'Bobby.' It's amazing!"

Two quietly spoken questions came from within the branches.

"*What made you do that, Bobby?*"

"*Did he really understand you?*"

Then in a slightly louder voice came a third question, "*Is he part bulb?*" Immediately, all of the bulbs started to laugh at Bingo's question, and the branches shook slightly.

When the laughing stopped, Bingo asked, "*Do you really think it's possible? Is he part bulb, Bobby?*" And then, the tree branches shook even harder.

Remington lay on his left side, and the top of the sheet and bedcover were pulled up to his shoulder.

His mom had just finished singing the first verse of "Silent Night," and he had already fallen asleep. She held her hand against his right cheek to see if he felt extra hot. There seemed to be no fever.

She leaned down, gave him one more kiss, and then she stood up. When she turned to go to the door, she looked directly at the tiny tree on the table, and her mouth flew open in disbelief.

Remington's mom and dad sat side–by–side on the edge of the bed. This was the second year in a row they had stayed in the downstairs bedroom, where Richard had slept from the day he was born until he graduated from high school.

Last year when Mr. and Mrs. McGillicuddy had given Remington his very own Christmas tree, Remington got to move to the upstairs bedroom. The McGillicuddys had purchased a queen–size bed for Richard's old bedroom, which replaced the small twin–size bed that had been there for over 30 years.

Even so, the room still looked a lot like it had in Richard's teenage years, with many of his basketball trophies and special awards scattered on the shelf, window seat, the triple–drawer dresser, and nightstand.

"I heard the noise upstairs while I was in the bathroom brushing my teeth."

"You did?"

"Yes. What's wrong with you? You've got a weird look on your face. Remington is okay, right?"

"Oh, yeah, he's fine."

"Honey," he put his left arm around her shoulder and pulled her into him. "He will be okay. It's a slight concussion. The fact he felt dizzy after getting out of bed is not that strange. You did say it happened because he got out of bed too quickly, didn't you?"

"Yes, I did. You are right. He will be fine."

"Lisa, are you listening to me? You're acting as if you're the one with a concussion. Look at me!"

She turned to him and smiled. "I'm okay, dear," she said, "even though our son believes he hears a Christmas tree light bulb talking to him, believes the bulb has winked at him, believes this bulb called 'Bobby' talks with the other bulbs on the tree, and believes the bulb flew downstairs and got Rocket to make enough noise so that your dad came into the house and found Remington. And, oh yes, before I forget, thanks to your dad, Remington believes that these bulbs saved your mom's life during the tornado.

"So, darling, I'm feeling so good that I'm now able to tell you that even I believe in magic and miracles. You see, now I've actually seen those bulbs make the tree branches shake." And then she explained what had happened.

It was quiet. The room was dark except for the ray of light from the full moon, which filtered through the top of the front window. Bobby could easily make out the form of Remington lying in bed a few feet away.

He could hear him breathing, and he heard him snore a couple of times. The rest of the bulbs were asleep. It had been a few hours since Remington's mom had turned off the lights when she left the room. Normally when Bobby's body cooled off, it was easy to go to sleep, but not tonight. He was wide-awake because every few minutes he would again start laughing when he remembered Bingo's joke. The bulbs had laughed so hard the tree branches had actually moved up and down. It happened just as Remington's mom had stood up and looked directly at the tree.

He smiled as he thought of the shocked look on her face. She had put both her hands over her eyes and then peeked back through her fingers, as if she was hoping she hadn't really seen the tree branches shaking.

"*Wow! That was so funny!*" He laughed again as he pictured the expression on her face, her mouth wide open in disbelief. She had quickly turned the Christmas tree lights off and hurried out of the room and down the stairs.

"*Oh, my goodness!*" Bobby said, "*What a year we've had and what a different Christmas!*"

31

More Shocking News

Remington turned the tree lights on the moment he awoke. He looked at the clock. It was 7:30 Christmas morning. He didn't hear any noises yet, but he was sure it wouldn't be very long before his grandpa would yell that Santa Claus had left some gifts downstairs.

But right now, all he wanted to do was enjoy his Christmas tree and the bright shining lights. "Good morning, my very special Christmas tree lights."

He turned the light switch on the wall to on and the lights glowed brightly. Now he stood directly in front of the tree, and he bent over to put his nose right up against the tip of the blue bulb.

"How are you doing, Bobby?"

Bobby felt the nose of Remington against his body. *Should I or shouldn't I*, he thought.

"*No matter what you are thinking right now, don't do it,*" his mom whispered to him.

"*Okay, Mom, I'll be good. But I wish I could tickle his nose.*"

"*Don't you even think about it,*" she ordered.

Remington finally pulled his nose away from the bulb, straightened himself, and stared at the tree for a few minutes.

Then he reached underneath the front branches of the tree and pulled a small wrapped box from the table. He had put it there when he arrived a few days ago. It was a gift from his 10-year old friend Blake, who lived next door to him. "He's my other good buddy, just like you, Bobby," he said, looking right at the blue bulb.

Remington had promised his friend he would wait until Christmas morning to unwrap the present, and his friend had promised him he would also wait until Christmas morning to open Remington's gift.

"Hey! This is neat," he said, as he removed the wrapping paper. "This looks like a fun game."

But before he could open the box and read the instructions, he heard the voice of his grandfather.

"Remington, I think somebody in a red and white suit came to the house last night. I see some gifts from someone named Santa Claus."

"All right, Grandpa, I'm on my way."

He put his newly opened present on the bed and turned to dash out the door. But he suddenly stopped, turned, and with a huge grin, which made the freckles on his face almost pop up in the air, he yelled, "Merry Christmas, Bobby, and make sure all of your family has a wonderful Christmas too!"

Then he ran out of the room, hurried down the stairs, and a few moments later the first of many squeals of excitement were heard.

"He just wished us Merry Christmas," Bobby said, *"So, let's have one!"* And suddenly the sound of 'Merry Christmas' in 'Bulbese' echoed throughout the tree.

It was a wonderful Christmas. The food was superb. Remington ate a few bites of turkey, some of his grandma's corn that he loved so much, picked over the other vegetables, and then ate three of her famous devilled eggs. Then he got to do what was allowed only once a year. He was given, not one, not two, but three pieces of pie. Each one, he had promised his grandmother, was his favorite.

"I mean it, Grandma," he said. "Each one is my favorite. Right now it is cherry," and he took the final bite of the flaky crust. Before Mrs. McGillicuddy could say anything, Remington laughed and told her, "and now my favorite is blueberry," and he took a big bite of the sugared berries. "Oh, that is so good," he said.

Five minutes later, he said the same thing about the piece of apple pie, which took a little bit longer to eat.

After dinner, the family played touch football in the backyard. Rocket added some noise and excitement. He chased the ball, barked at everyone, and tried to knock down whoever was running with the football.

When the game was over, everyone returned inside. Mrs. McGillicuddy laughed and said, "Here, Rocket, this turkey leg bone is for you."

"Why does he get the turkey leg, Grandma?" Remington asked. "It's his reward for the most tackles in the game," she said, and chuckled. .

Everyone laughed and the fun–filled atmosphere continued throughout the day. But there was some shocking news waiting for Mr. and Mrs. McGillicuddy when it was bedtime for Remington.

"Can't we stay a couple of more days like we did last Christmas?"

"We've been through this, Remington," his mom said. "You know Daddy has to be back at work the day after tomorrow. We have to leave early in the morning, so get to sleep."

"Yes, close those eyes and go to sleep, my little buddy," Mr. McGillicuddy said as he walked into the room.

"I'll miss you, Grandpa," Remington said, and he sat up in bed and held his hands out in front of him. "Come give me a goodnight kiss."

"Am I going to get one too?"

Remington saw his grandmother standing in the doorway, smiling.

"Yep! I have one for both of you."

"Do we have to share just one kiss?" his grandpa joked.

"No, you get at least one each," Remington laughed.

"Well, don't forget me, Remington," his dad said as he walked into the room.

"Okay, Daddy, I'll save you one."

After all the hugs and kisses were completed, Remington said, "I'm going to miss Christmas here so much next year."

"Remington!"

"What, Daddy?"

Before Remington's father could answer, Mrs. McGillicuddy said, "What do you mean by that, Remington?"

And then, there was silence.

Remington looked at his dad, and then he looked at his mom, and then at his grandparents. It was Mrs. McGillicuddy who frowned and finally said, "This doesn't sound very good. What's going on here?"

"Well, I will miss you next Christmas, Grandma, and you too, Grandpa, and all of my friends on the tree, and especially Bobby."

Now Mr. McGillicuddy had a worried look. "That does it! Will someone tell me what this means?"

Remington's dad put his arm around his mom and said, "Well, I guess the time has come. Lisa and I kind of had it planned differently. We were going to tell you in the morning, but I guess we will tell you now."

"Don't be angry at me, Daddy, please!"

"I'm not angry, Remington. Shoot, I will miss them too."

"Stop all this nonsense, right now," yelled Mr. McGillicuddy. "Tell us what's going on."

It took a few moments for Richard to get a chair from the nearby office, bring it to the room, and set it just inside the doorway. Then he told Mrs. McGillicuddy to sit down.

Remington remained in bed, with his mom sitting next to him. Mr. McGillicuddy was in the chair by the window and Remington's Dad, after having arranged everyone's position, stood in the middle of the room.

"I have a special assignment that's been given to me, and we are moving to Spain."

"Well, you could have taken a few more seconds to explain some of the reasons before just blurting out the news, Richard," Lisa interjected.

No one said anything for nearly ten seconds, and then Mrs. McGillicuddy started to cry.

"You mean you're not going to live in the United States ever again?" she asked, and more tears rolled down her cheeks.

"Oh, Mother, don't be so dramatic. I'm being sent for a year to work at the U.S. Embassy in Madrid and to do some special assignments for our government."

"Oh, Richard, I'm so proud of you," and she wiped tears off her face.

"It is a great opportunity," Lisa added.

"Well, I'll be," Mr. McGillicuddy chipped in, "my son, the international diplomat."

"Not really, Dad! Mostly behind the scenes work inside the embassy. We will live there about two years."

"You said only a year, a moment ago."

"That's probably right, Mom" he answered. "We should get most of the work done in just over a year, possibly 18 months, and so there is a good chance we will be back here at home for Christmas two years from now."

"But it just won't be the same without you here. Can't you come home for Christmas? I mean, you do get a vacation, don't you?"

"Yes, but there are some things that the embassy will want done in December that will keep us from traveling."

"Don't cry, Grandma." Remington slid out from underneath the sheet and blanket. He got out of bed and walked carefully to her side, looked up at her, and said, "I've got a great idea!"

"Really, it's more than an idea," Lisa said, "It's actually a surprise from the three of us."

"I was going to tell them," Remington interrupted, "Can't I please tell them, Mom?"

32

And Then, the Good News

"Well, all of this has been a surprise, so what else can happen?" Mrs. McGillicuddy asked.

"We have a little something extra for both of you," Lisa answered.

"Mom, you said I could give it to them."

"I know. I just wanted them to understand."

"Lisa," Remington's dad interrupted, "Let him get the tickets."

"Dad! You're giving away the secret."

"What's going on with you three?" Mr. McGillicuddy cut in as he stood up in front of his chair.

Remington pushed by his grandpa and ran out of the room and down the stairs.

"Slow down, Remington," his dad pleaded. "No more accidents." Then, he looked at the other three and laughed. "I guess that sore head and concussion are better."

The others chuckled, and then they all looked at each other. No one knew what to say, so they said nothing for nearly a minute until Remington raced back into the room.

"Not so fast, Remington," Lisa warned. "Take it easy!"

His hands were behind his back. "Close your eyes, Grandma."

She did as she was told. "What kind of surprise do you have for me?"

"Oh, it's for both of you."

"Me too?" Mr. McGillicuddy asked.

"Close your eyes right now, Grandpa."

He did as he was told.

Remington placed both of his hands in front of him. His right arm was extended toward his grandma, his left arm toward his grandpa.

He made the sound of a drum roll and said, "Ta da."

But his grandparents still had their eyes closed.

"Ta da," he said it one more time. "Okay! Open up your eyes." Remington handed Mrs. McGillicuddy a closed folder. "This one is yours, Grandma."

"Thank you."

"And, this is your ticket, Grandpa."

"My what?" Mr. McGillicuddy asked.

"Just open it up, Grandpa. You will see."

"Is this what I think it is?" Mrs. McGillicuddy was looking at an American Airlines ticket jacket.

Then Remington, acting like one of those television game show hosts, threw his arms out to both sides, and with hands upward, proclaimed loudly, "Ladies and gentlemen. Sit back and get comfortable. You are going to Spain for Christmas."

"Really? You mean it?" Mr. McGillicuddy stood up, opened the folder, and saw his ticket.

Mrs. McGillicuddy was already clutching her ticket like it was gold.

"We had to get the embassy to pull some strings so we could buy this a year in advance. But it was part of my agreement to come do this special job for them."

"Oh, Richard," Mrs. McGillicuddy hugged her son. "And you too, Lisa." She reached over and embraced her daughter-in-law. "Both of you are so wonderful."

Mr. McGillicuddy stood watching with tears rolling down the front of his face.

"Grandpa," Remington asked, "Are you okay?"

Everyone turned and looked at Mr. McGillicuddy.

"I'm just fine, Remington, but I think there must be a leak in the roof. There's water dripping on my cheeks."

Then everyone laughed, and there was lots of hugging and kissing.

"We are going to be in Spain for Christmas."

"Yes, we are, dear," Mr. McGillicuddy said, "and that water from the ceiling must be dripping on you, too."

<u>Epilogue</u>

Bobby could hear everyone talking downstairs as Remington and his parents took their luggage out the front door and to the SUV in the driveway.

He recalled telling the news to the rest of the bulbs last night after Remington was asleep.

"Oh, Bobby," his mom was crying. "*Now this means we will be locked up in that closet for almost two years.*"

His dad even sounded choked up. "*I can't believe this either. Here you save me from being thrown away, and now we're going to be stuck in that dark closet for two years.*"

"*This is unacceptable,*" bellowed Uncle Flicker.

"*Bobby, you have to do something,*" pleaded Dimmer. "*You be the bulb, Bobby. You have to save us. Don't let us be buried in that closet for two years. Why can't we go to Spain?*"

"*I know you will find a way to do it, Bobby,*" his mom encouraged him.

Next door to his left, Aunt Glaring twisted and leaned toward him. She clinked against him.

"*You have eleven months to figure out a way to get us there,*" she said with a smile. "*I know you will think of something.*"

Bobby winked and said, "*I always do.*" Then he yelled, "*Okay! Christmas in Spain,*" and the Bright family cheered loudly.

Bobby's thoughts of last night were interrupted when he heard Remington, from outside the front door, shouting goodbye to his grandparents.

Soon Mr. McGillicuddy would come upstairs and begin taking the ornaments and the strand of lights off the tree. Bobby hoped what he had done last night, while Remington was asleep, would not be discovered.

Through more of his magical stunts, he had managed to return his dad and cousin Whitening to their own pods. The Bobby Bright family was still together. By the end of the day, they would all be in the closet again.

"It's okay, Jane. We'll call them tonight and make sure they got home safely."

"I know. I just miss them already."

The front door closed, and the McGillicuddys continued to talk while upstairs the world's most amazing Christmas tree light bulb was deep in thought. *Will we really spend Christmas in Spain? Can I really make it happen?*

Special words and phrases in "bulbese"

"Bulbese" is a very special language and it is impossible to translate more than a few words or phrases into human language.

Bobby Bright has been able to assist author John Brooks as he tries to learn a few words.

Following are the only known "Bulbese" words or sounds that can be understood by humans. Mr. Brooks is the only human who can understand the following sounds. Of course, Remington McGillicuddy will one day have a chance to learn these words, and maybe even more, in the fourth book in the series, *Bobby Bright Becomes a Professor.*

The "Bulbese" phrases and sentences are printed in dark letters. The pronunciation is in parentheses ( ). See the pronunciation key to say each word correctly. The meaning of each entry follows its pronunciation.

Beep' — de — — beep' — —eee (bēp' di bēp' ē>),
MERRY CHRISTMAS!

Beep' — —uhh — de' — — beep (bēp' ə di' bēp), **WHAT IS
YOUR NAME?**

B–e–e–p/beep' de (bē>pbep> di),
MY NAME IS ... .

Beep .... Beep .... Beep/Beep?' (bēp> bēp>bēpbēp'?), **HOW
OLD ARE YOU?**

B–e–e–e–e–e–e–p ... ... Bee .... Beep (bē>ē>p> bē> bēp),
ARE YOU HAPPY?

B–e–e–e–p (pause) B–e–e–e–p (pause) Beep — de — —Beep?'
(bē>p % bē>p % bē>pdibēp?),
WHAT TIME IS IT?

B–e–e–e–p (pause) B–e–e–e–p (pause) B–e–e–e–e–p (pause)
B–e–e–e–e–e–e–p beep/beep'? (bē>p % bē>p % bē>ē>p %
bē>ē>ē>p bēpbēp'?), **DO YOU LIKE SCHOOL?**

Beep B–e–e–e–e–e–e–e–e–e–e–e–p B–e–e–e–p (bēp
bē>ē>ē>ē>p bē>p), **I LOVE YOU.**

B–e–e–e–p de' b–e–e–e–p de' beep/beep (bē>p di' bē>p di'
bēpbēp), **HAPPY BIRTHDAY!**

Beep/Beep B–e–e–e–e–p (bēpbēp bē>ē>p),
LET'S PLAY A GAME.

John Brooks is a semi-retired sportscaster and owner of Sportscast Productions, Inc., a 36-year old company involved in radio and television sports productions and sports advertising. He is a past vice-president of the National Sportswriters & Sportscaster Association, and winner of the Coca-Cola/PowerAde National Sportscast of the Year Award in 2000. With nearly 2,900 professional and collegiate play-by-play broadcasts on his resume, his many credits include, "Voice" of the University of Oklahoma Basketball and Football radio networks for 16 years and the "Voice" of the Oklahoma City Blazers and San Diego Gulls professional hockey teams for 28 seasons. He is married to Lisa, has three children, Remington, Stacey, and Angie, and lives in Oklahoma City and part-time in Madrid, Spain.

Coming in the near future:
"Bobby Bright Spends Christmas in Spain"
"Bobby Bright Becomes a Professor"
"Bobby Bright Meets His Maker"

Other Bobby Bright books
"Bobby Bright's Greatest Christmas Ever"